MVFOL

D0031767

BLOOD HARVEST

A NOVEL

BLOOD HARVEST

BRANT RANDALL

CAPITAL CRIME PRESS
FORT COLLINS, COLORADO

This is a work of fiction. Names, characters, places, and incidents are the products of the author's imagination or are used fictitiously. Any resemblance to actual events, locales, or persons, living or dead, is entirely coincidental.

Copyright © 2008 by Brant Randall

All rights reserved. No part of this book may be used or reproduced in any manner whatsoever without written permission except in the case of brief quotations in critical reviews or articles. For information address Capital Crime Press, P.O. Box 272904, Fort Collins, CO 80527

First edition published in the United States by Capital Crime Press. Printed in Canada.

Capital Crime Press is a registered trademark.

LCCN: 2008921433
ISBN-13: 978-0-9799960-1-6
ISBN-10: 0-9799960-1-5

www.capitalcrimepress.com

For sweet Robin

I want to acknowledge my debt to my fellow writers RB, SL, and GF. Their scrutiny and careful reading of the early drafts greatly improved this book. A special thanks to editor extraordinaire, Alex Cole.

1929

The past is a foreign land.
Things are done differently there.

A note from the author

This novel grew from an incident related to me by my grandmother when she was in her nineties. She was a Scotch-Irish girl from rural New England, one of twelve children, though two died in infancy.

I knew she had married young, perhaps at sixteen, though she sometimes claimed she had been eighteen. She said that after her wedding day she never returned to her hometown. I assumed that she eloped or otherwise angered her parents. At one point I asked if her parents disliked my grandfather, who I remembered as personable and charming.

She claimed that they liked him very much. He was a perfect example of the immigrant success story. Came to America from Greece at sixteen, without any English. Started working the next day. Within five years he owned his own restaurant, and in another five he added a chain of candy shops and drug stores.

"So why didn't you ever return to your hometown?"

"It was those dumb clucks." She used this expression only when quite angry. "My brother-in-law didn't think it right for a white girl to marry a non-white European."

This was new territory to me, but when I read my grandfather's immigration papers I found that Southern Europeans—the Greeks, Spanish, Italians, and Turks— were classified thus until 1912. But it was her next revelation that stunned me.

It wasn't dumb "clucks." It was dumb "klux." My grandparents had been driven from the town by the Ku Klux Klan. This was not consistent with what I had learned in my history classes, and so I began to research.

In 1915 the KKK had been moribund for forty years. It was then revived as an anti-immigrant, anti-Catholic movement, though with plenty of hatred and racism left over for blacks. It was centered not in the South, but in the Northeast, with a large contingent in the Midwest.

Since I have family alive who recall these incidents and still live in the area, the names and locations have been changed. This is a work of fiction loosely based on several actual events.

I also learned that the Klan, in a variety of new forms, is still very much active.

Brant Randall

MARSHAL LAWE

By the *sword* we seek peace,
but peace only under liberty.
— *Massachusetts state motto*

Uh-huh.
— *Marshal Lawe*

I.

SOME SAY THAT I'm quarrelsome. Others hold that I'm a gossip. Fact is, I'm just interested in the truth, me being sworn to uphold the law. I take the workings of justice serious.

So let me tell you about the time I was riding herd on six members of the MacKay family, trying to keep them on the bench out in the courthouse hallway, waiting their turn to testify in the Angus DeCosta case. Big Bill Sykes, the prosecuting attorney, was calling it aggravated assault and attempted murder on Angus.

It turns out Angus is cousin to every one of the MacKays. His ma's name was Mary Elizabeth MacKay before she eloped with that wop "grocer," Nick DeCosta. It looked to be a troublesome case, what with half the county related to the defendants.

About four years before I become a marshal in Peony Springs—I guess that would have been the summer of 1916—the MacKays had got the Ku Klux Klan after Nick DeCosta, account of they didn't want no non-white European courting their girl Mary Elizabeth. One night they treed Nick like he was some Eye-talian coon and was fixing to make him sing soprano, when Mary Elizabeth drives up in her daddy's Model T which she's gone and pinched out of the barn. She shines the headlights on her family, jerks an M97 shotgun from the floorboard, draws down, and tells them she's carrying Nick's bambino.

Since Nick was twenty-two and she was not quite fifteen there was a certain amount of concern-ation among her brothers and uncles, though the other klucks didn't see how it altered the case. Some were of a mind that she didn't really know how to use the shotgun, and others were just as sure she did.

A few thought they should overpower her in a quick rush, beat some sense into her, and maybe the beating would rid her of the baby at the same time. Others thought you ought to protect "the little mother."

After lively debate, they all agreed that whatever way the MacKays dealt with their wayward girl was purely a family matter. And irregardless, Nick and his balls was still going to have to part company.

That's when Mary Elizabeth began firing. The way I heard it, she couldn't aim worth a dang, and the kick of the 12 gauge jerked the barrel around every direction but straight. But she kept firing the pump-action and made them all dance pretty vigorous while her boyfriend climbed down, jumped into the driver's seat, and they skedaddled.

In the end they made it across the county line, and never set foot back in Potemkin County.

II.

A little learning is a dangerous thing
Drink deep, or taste not the Pierian spring
There shallow draughts intoxicate the brain,
And drinking deep largely sobers us again.
— *Alexander Pope*

EVERYTHING CONSIDERED, I'M lucky I got my job as dep'ty marshal when I did. At that time in Potemkin all that was required was some high school, or being a veteran of the Great War. Now that it's 1929 and being modern times, they're making the new guys take a year of college classes to learn "Principles of Law Enforcement."

Problem is them college high-brow professors ain't never set foot inside a real courthouse. They don't know how to serve a process, or transport a felon, or keep witnesses orderly, or how to cuff someone who don't wanna be cuffed, or what have you.

I'm sure you take my meaning. Lack of experience. Probably think criminals can be rehabilitated or some such, which is just so much horse hockey. After you work the courthouse ten years, you know better.

There's a reason they call it the penitentiary and not the rehabilitory. Only thing going to habilitate most of these aye-holes is a nightstick upside their ear-hole.

Listening to some of these defense attorneys—and most

likely they went to the same college that teaches those law enforcement pimples—watching them weep and boo-hoo and carry on in front of the judge and jury makes me want to vomit. I'm happy to say I got my education right here in the halls of justice. And it's mostly in the halls, not the courtrooms, that the real justice happens.

Which brings me back to Angus DeCosta, the boy that Mary Elizabeth birthed fifteen years ago. Back then Mary Elizabeth had Nick curled tight around her pinky, and it was her idea to give the baby the same name as her daddy, hoping that would heal the breach betwixt the families.

Course it did no such thing, and the DeCostas and MacKays kept on their respectable sides of Euphrates Crick, which serves as the county line. Nick was worried that the Klan didn't have the same exact jurisdictional boundaries and he didn't have no family to back him up—him being nimmigrant and all—so he made sure he contributed plenty to the Jefferson County Sheriff's re-election campaign and always kept a loaded gun nearby.

Things had remained settled for some time, but once Angus hit pub-berty he begin running wild. He crossed into Potemkin County on a dare, showing up at a covered dish church sociable where a lot of MacKays was in attendance.

None of them had ever seen him before, so there wasn't no problem until he was spied snuggling with Jackie Sue in the rhododendrons. Each of them had their hands inside the other's clothes. Jackie's older cousin run into the shrubbery bellowing like a bull and got a grip on Angus' ear. He commenced to pulling, demanding the kid's name.

By pure ornery luck Jackie's cousin was also named Angus. He'd been named after the pater familias. So when the DeCosta boy said that he was Angus he thought the kid was sassing him.

By the time it was over Angus DeCosta's ear wasn't never going to be right again, and of course it didn't help that Angus MacKay had lost some two cubic inches from the fleshy part of his leg, due to his not believing that a fifteen-year-old could have teeth that sharp.

Which reminds me that Judge Halbertson has taken to calling this the case of the two An-guy, thinking he's made some kind of clever joke about the plural form of Angus. He took one semester of Latin in high school and now he thinks he's omnivorous.

Yep, he's a card all right, a regular Will Rogers. He pretends my name is pretty funny. Not Ichabod, that's my first name, but Lawe. Says it don't take Marshal Lawe to keep order in Peony Springs, civil law is just fine.

Anyhow, back to the particulars. The MacKay menfolk give the DeCosta boy a right good drubbing, stripped him bare, and drove him to the county line bridge, where they threw him into the Euphrates. The bridge is more than thirty feet above the water and the water ain't that deep, maybe ten feet.

Angus broke one leg hitting the bottom hard and sprained the other ankle. On top of which he couldn't swim any better than a dog paddle, so he was near drownt.

About the same time Nick DeCosta drives up to the bridge from the Jefferson County side. Mary Elizabeth had been worried sick that her boy might have run away, or maybe he fell in a ditch, or perhaps he'd fallen among evil companions and was drinking jake.

You know the way mothers can carry on. Finally, out

of self-defense, Nick had jumped in his car and gone looking for the kid. Wanted out of the house as much as anything.

He saw a bunch of MacKay menfolk hanging over the bridge rail, a-taunting someone in the water, realized it's his own boy down there, and maybe he begun to relive his past. He took example from Mary Elizabeth, jerked the shotgun out of the back of his pickup truck, and opened fire. 'Twas only 20 gauge because he'd been hunting duck and pheasant of late, but he put plenty of birdshot into the hides of the MacKays, providing cover while his boy dragged hisself out of the water.

It took a few minutes to get the wounded MacKays into their own vehicles and decide who needed to be sent back to the Potemkin County hospital, but finally the MacKays gave chase, crossing over into Jefferson County.

By the time they caught up to the DeCostas, they were right in front of the Sheriff's station. Officer Dopey—his real name's Dobro, since he's Yugoslovakian or some such—Officer Dopey come out and tried to arrest everyone. Things developed into a general brawl that was put to an an end when Dopey fired a few rounds into the air.

Couple days later, after the ee-lected Sheriff of Potemkin County got on the telephone to the ee-lected Sheriff of Jefferson County, it was decided that the first case was going to be tried in the Potemkin courthouse since the original fracas between the two Anguses had taken place in our county, while the original attempted murder—by which I mean when they threw the nekkid DeCosta boy off the bridge—happened on the Potemkin side of the river.

In Jefferson County Nick DeCosta was charged with a

second attempted murder. By birdshot, no less. Based on his donation record to the Sheriff's re-election campaign, I think that one's going to go moot, which is a legal term means the court'll just hush up about it.

Meanwhile Nick was enjoying Potemkin County hospitality in the holding cell across the street, waiting for his turn to testify against the MacKays.

You have to wonder at this whole justice system. You got the Sheriff being put in office because he's got more blood relatives than the guy running against him, then the judge getting chose just the same way, plus you got the moonshiners and your other successful businessmen making sure the both of them have healthy campaign funds. I mean, where's somebody going to get justice if they ain't connected?

I figure I'm part of the solution to that die-lemma. I'm the man that can help the little guy get some justice. Suppose a body realizes that some particular piece of evidence is likely to make him to look bad. If they can convince me that they didn't actually do the crime, I can help that bit disappear from the storage area. Judges have their hands tied, what with all these "rules of evidence." So much so that they can't always see justice done.

On occasion I'll have a lawyer wants to make sure who's going to get put in the jury pool. I do a quick read through of the names on the list, maybe tell the clerk which ones are "sick" or "out of town" or whatever. Sometimes it requires hand-picking to gar-rantee an anonymous verdict.

III.

No gossip ever dies away entirely…
It is a kind of divinity.
Works and Days
— *Hesiod*

ANYWAYS, IT WAS too noisy in the hallway and I tried to quieten the MacKays down, telling them it wasn't no quilting bee. But they were riled up because of what they'd heard through the door to the courtroom.

I have to admit that this was partly my fault. I'd had the door ajar and my head poked in so I could listen.

It's always useful if I pick up some bit of testimony that I can pass on to the right party, and the sale of such information helps pad out the poor salary I receive as an officer of the court. Besides, I had an interest in the case. I not only knowed most of the principals, but also had come upon some facts concerning the DeCostas' affairs in Jefferson County as well.

The person testifying was Mrs. Harmon, half MacKay by blood, and maybe a questionable source. She testified as to Angus MacKay's behavior leading up to the assault, having been an eyewitness to the whole thing. She's also one hunnerd per cent busybody, gossip, and mean mouth, no matter that her husband has been deacon at Mount Carmel Baptist for thirty-two years.

She had one of them voices that penetrated. It was whiny and nasal and felt like an ice pick going into your ear.

And the orange hair. Somehow her best friends hadn't told her she ought not to mix peroxide and henna into her old gray locks. Plus, those locks had been marcelled near to death. The jury stared at her like they was at the circus sideshow, and Mrs. Harmon was none too pleased over it. She gave it a screechy emphasis when she said it was her opinion that Angus MacKay didn't have the brains or sense of a medium squirrel.

The MacKays sitting out in the hall couldn't hear clearly. Some realized she was talking about one of the two An-guy, but others thought she was speaking ill of Angus MacKay, the clan patriarch, dead these last five years, and that set them buzzing. I shushed them, then poked my head back inside.

That's when I saw the judge motion to the bailiff. Next thing I know the bailiff is headed right for me. I figured I was going to catch some heck from the judge, like that time I asked if he was going to have some moonshiners pay their fine in cash or goods.

The sawed-off son of a bachelor had called me impotent right in front of the whole court, and said he wasn't going to tolerate my impotence any further. Told the bailiff that from now on I was not to step foot inside the courtroom unless a shackled suspect needed escorting back to the jail.

As it happened this time, the bailiff was only bringing me the judge's luncheon order. Prohibition being the law of the land, the judge didn't think he should be seen drinking in public, so he always had me pick up his noon meal from the diner across the street and leave it beside the rear entry to his chambers. That way he could knock back a couple of stiff ones in private. The meatloaf and potatoes would soak it up before he reconvenienced the jury.

I made my way across the street and placed the judge's order. Hadn't been there more than two minutes when Big Bill Sykes sidled up next to me at the counter. He called out his order for a turkey on white and winked at Gladys—she's the one with the lazy eye, makes up the sammiches at lunchtime—telling her he'd appreciate it if she went light on the mayo but heavy on the turkey, maybe he'd give her a heavier tip.

Gladys looked right back at him and winked at him with her lazy eye—not her good one—muttered something under her breath sounded like "chizzler." Sykes acted like he didn't hear it, but I'm sure he did.

I looked over at Big Bill, couldn't remember that I'd ever seen him in the diner before. He always took his lunch at the hotel restaurant. Bill looked right back at me.

"You got a horse in this race?" said Sykes.

"I don't follow you," I said.

"I had a heckuva time finding enough jury members not related to Angus and Andrew MacKay. Perhaps you might have had something to do with that."

"I'm only the marshal, counselor. I've nothing to do with the jury pool."

"I'm just trying to determine the lay of the land. This is an important case, and I think I have it all sewn up. The testimony is pretty clear."

I held my peace. I knew Sykes was planning to run for the Senate, and he thought that a strong showing in this case would make him look good to the state's reform vote.

Sykes gave it another try. "Is the public defender going to spring any surprises, Marshal?"

I shook my head, neither confirming nor denying the possibility. Gladys came around the counter with the judge's lunch on a foil-covered plate. I looked away from Sykes and said, "Put this on the judge's tab, will ya?"

Gladys waved her hand in disgust. "Who you trying to fool, Icky? Hizz-onner never pays that tab."

Sykes looked back and forth between me and Gladys. "Icky?"

I spun on my heel and marched out of there before Big Bill got started on the Icky jokes. Folks have a hard time leaving my name alone.

IV.

The hungry judges soon the sentence sign,
And wretches hang that jurymen may dine.
    The Rape of the Lock
        — *Alexander Pope*

I TOOK THE judge's meal across the street. His chambers had a rear entry that opened onto a small street at the side of the courthouse. Chief, our town's police dog, was already there, having found a nice spot in the shade, hoping to lap up the judge's leftovers.

To my surprise the door was ajar. I stood there a moment deciding whether to knock or just drop off the food, when I heard Judge Halbertson's voice.

"You should have thought of that before you pulled your dress up for him. You made your own bed and now you have to lie in it."

There was the low sound of a woman's voice and then a crash of glass. The door burst open and there she was, blinking in the sunlight, waiting for her eyes to adjust, her face a study in anxiety.

At fourteen Mary Elizabeth had been cute as a button, what with her Scotch-Irish blue eyes and skin so fair it was near translucent. Now that she was twenty-nine she had ripened into a fine-looking woman.

She and Nick had only had the one boy, and there was some talk of why Nick had never sired another on her. Some said he wanted her to keep her figure, others opined that maybe she'd been too young the first time and couldn't have no more. And those with the sharpest tongues said that even the first one wasn't Nick's at all, that he never did have any lead in his pencil.

If you were to ask my thinking on the subject, I'd say Angus was Nick's boy all right. He had his dad's eyes and general look, though his skin coloring was an interesting mix of olive and fair. Gave him a bit more of color in the cheeks and lips than his momma had. Yessir, the boy was a study in the fruits of miss-skidge-anation.

I brushed past Mary Elizabeth and put the judge's lunch inside the door. He must have thought it was her coming back because he shouted out, "And you owe me another case of Nick's best!"

I closed the door on him and took Mary Elizabeth by the elbow, to steer her into the shade, get her out of sight. She jerked away with a little sound of pain and I saw that there were fresh bruises on her arm. Looked like someone with big hands had squeezed pretty hard.

I gestured that she follow me into the alley between the courthouse and the city hall. "I don't think you want to be seen out on the street. Too many MacKays around."

She stepped into the deep shadows and leaned against the wall, brushing at her eyes, flicking away tears. Whether they were tears of anger or frustration or pain I weren't sure. Looking at her more closely I saw the greenish-blue marks of older bruises on both arms—even some on her calves.

"You done with your inspection, Marshal? Don't you know it's not polite to stare like that?"

Her voice had deepened some since I last heard it, wasn't a girl's voice no more. But it sounded nice to my ear, kind of warm and musical, even though there was a deal of strain in it at the moment.

"Didn't mean to offend you, Mary Eliz...ma'am. I'm just thinking on how I can get you safely back to Jefferson County. You don't want to be meeting your kinfolk, not with them as angered as they are."

Mary Elizabeth stared at me for a long moment, till I began to feel uncomfortable myself. "I know you, don't I? You went to high school with my oldest brother, but then you shipped off with the Navy."

"That's right. I did know Scott some," I said.

"I don't recall your name, though I recollect it was something unusual."

I felt my coloring come up and was angry that it'd done so. "Ichabod Lawe."

For the first time her expression lightened a bit. "I remember now. The girls called you Icky back then."

"Some still do."

"What's your middle name?"

"Petrarch. My daddy read a book by him, thought the world of the man's literary skills."

"That won't do either. What if I used just your initials?" She thought for a second and I thought I saw a bit of a smile flash across her face. "No, I see that has its own problems. Well, I believe I'll just call you Marshal."

"Listen, ma'am, enjoyable as—"

"It's Mary."

"Mary, as enjoyable as this conversation has been, I'm concerned for your safety."

"Hadn't you heard about my exploits with a shotgun? I can take care of myself."

"I believe you should get on back to Jefferson County," I said.

"I'm not going back until I can take my boy with me."

"And why is that?"

"I fear to leave him in this town overnight. I'm not sure the law can protect him here."

I waited for her to go on, but she just looked at me.

"You also concerned about your husband Nick being here overnight?" I said.

Something flickered across her face.

"Sure. Nick, too."

V.

God is a comedian
playing to an audience
too afraid to laugh.
— *Voltaire*

I HAD HER wait in the cloakroom in the basement of
the courthouse, getting her in through a delivery door
that was down a stairwell, below street level. Told her
I'd personally drive her home later that night. I gave her
the sack lunch I'd brought for myself, then went back to
the diner and put another meal on the judge's tab, telling
Gladys that hizz-onner had liked the first one so much
he wanted a repeat. Gladys snorted and rolled her eyes
in different directions simultaneous.

By midafternoon, all the MacKays had spoken their
piece. After each one testified, they come out in the hall
looking glum. I moved them to a holding room in case
any of them might be recalled to the stand.

Come three o'clock I brought Angus DeCosta before
the bar in a wheelchair, pushed him right up in front of
the judge's bench. The whole room begin to buzz with
hostility, and the judge gaveled until his hand was sore,
trying to get some order in the court. Halbertson scowled
at me, then jerked his shoulder.

Me and the bailiff removed a couple of the more vocal

observers, including Old Lady MacKay, the clan matriarch. I grabbed her by her scrawny elbow but it felt more like I had hold of something electrical. She didn't weigh ninety pounds, stood four foot ten, but it was more work than roping livestock to get her out of the courtroom.

Once I had her in the hallway, she turned on me with a vicious glare that like to burn a hole in me.

"Ichabod Lawe, have you lost your senses? My grandsons need my presence in the courtroom. It reassures them that justice will be done."

"Miz MacKay, if the judge tells me to remove you from the court, I got to do it. And if you had hushed when he told you to—"

"That public defender attorney is incompetent. He cannot get Angus and Andrew off."

"You can wait out here in the hall if you want, but I suggest you go on home," I said. "When the court adjourns there's going to be a lot of hungry folk headed toward your house."

She stared at me for several seconds before she said, "What will it cost, Marshal? What will it take to get the judge to declare a mistrial or some such?"

"I'm going to pretend I didn't hear that, Miz MacKay. Trying to fix the outcome of a trial is a felonious crime, and I'm sure you don't intend no such thing."

"I will not be having my grandchildren going to jail, not in a county full of my own kin, not while I have breath to stop it."

She glared at me some more, then hurried out of the courthouse and down the street, like she'd remembered she had something to do. I didn't like to bear witness to her anger, but I didn't know what to do about it. And besides, I had to fetch Nick DeCosta.

Since Nick mighta could be indicted for attempted homicide, I was instructed to both shackle and handcuff him for the trip from the holding cell into the courtroom. He didn't take to it well, and told me so.

"You acting like one of Mussolini's fascisti," said Nick. "You treat me like I got no rights."

My dog, Chief, decided to join the conversation at that point. He didn't seem to care for Nick's tone. He let loose a deep-chested rumble like distant thunder.

"I don't like it for your dog to make the growling at me," said Nick.

I guess Chief understood that because he give out with a bark that sounded like coal going down a chute.

Nick decided to hold his tongue.

Chief's a 110 pound German shepherd, and the best member of the police force. Never gets drunk, doesn't come in late, no back talk. I told Nick that the dog was for his protection, not because I feared he might run off.

Still, it was no Sunday stroll getting Nick across the street. I thought a MacKay might show up any instant, decide to take the law into his own hands, and remove a key witness for the prosecution. I actually loosened my revolver in its holster.

Nick saw what I was doing and grew a shade or two paler, though it was hard to tell, considering the tan he had. I tried to take his mind off it as we crossed the exposed street.

"I got a cousin down Fremont way," I said. "He says you make the best 'shine in the county. Not only potent, but it has some extra bit of flavor that makes it go down smooth-like."

Nick looked at me, realizing I was trying to ease his mind. "All these Scotches and Irish think you make whiskey only with the corn or rye. But I like to put in some grape mash too, leave the skin and seeds there. That's what make it to have character."

"Grape mash? You don't say? I thought you only used that for wine."

"We make wine in Italy before there was a Scotland. We learned it from the Romans, and they learn it from the Etrusci."

We got into the courthouse hallway, and I helped him to a seat. I filed that little bit of shine know-how away for future use. I had the feeling someone new might have to take over Nick's still.

The prosecution called for Nick to testify at four o'clock. Just the sight of him caused some more courtroom uproar, and the bailiff and I had to hustle another three MacKays to the sidewalk. I stood there with my hand on my gun whilst they walked away, though they cast many a black look over their shoulders at me.

I walked Nick back to his holding cell near half past four. I watched careful-like to see if any of those I'd ejected had come back with some firepower, but no one showed.

Something was bothering me and as I locked Nick into the cell I said, "I saw a lot of bruises on Mary Elizabeth's arms."

Nick jumped to his feet, roaring mad, grabbed hold of the bars like he was trying to choke them. "How you know my wife's name? The puttana is mine. You stay away if you know what's good for you."

I don't cotton to back talk from people in a cell, so I put my nightstick across his knuckles. He dropped to the floor yowling, which woke Chief up. Chief began to bark, and between the two of them it was a regular opera. I left them to it and went back to the courthouse, thinking things over.

By half past five, the judge gave the case to the jury and told them they could begin deliberating the next morning. And of course they weren't to discuss it with each other or anybody else.

I've noticed juries don't usually listen so good to this last bit and I certainly heard plenty of discussion, most of it heated, as the jurors made their way out of the courthouse. Seemed to me the jurors were not happy that they might have to convict some of their neighbors, and put it down as the fault of Nick DeCosta, a man not even an American citizen.

The more fair-minded of them argued that Big Bill Sykes had done a bang up job showing that Angus MacKay and his brother Andrew did have actual intent to murder the DeCosta boy. It looked to me as if this case might stir things up countywide, stir it up in a dangerous way.

I waited until six when it was dusking, then fetched the county marshal car and helped Angus DeCosta into the back seat. I pulled the car into the alley and fetched Mary Elizabeth from the cloakroom. Chief took his nighttime post guarding the jail.

I drove out of town with the headlights off and as little noise as possible, not wanting to alert anybody as to our whereabouts. I left off the police radio to make sure nobody tried to call me back to town.

We got across the county line into Jefferson. It was an uneasy moment as we crossed the Euphrates bridge, what with Angus beginning to blubber as he remembered his near drowning just three days before. It caused Mary

Elizabeth to clutch onto my arm as she told the boy to hush. I steered into the first town we come to and treated the two of them to dinner.

Once at their house, I stayed awhile and talked of the old days in Potemkin County. Angus got bored and went on to bed. Mary Elizabeth and I reminisced some more over folks we had known back then, how her brother Scott had survived the war, but then was struck down by the influenza. She said she hadn't been allowed to go to his funeral.

"You mean your family wouldn't let you mourn your own brother?"

She shook her head.

"When they got word to me about the viewing and the wake, Nick went crazy mad. Told me I couldn't see them, not any of them, ever again."

"Well, that's a shame. That might have been the chance to reconcile with your folks."

She looked at me hard. "I bundled Angus into his winter clothes and we started to walk back to Peony Springs, hoping to hitch a ride with someone. Nick caught up to us some six miles down the road. Near beat me to death."

VI.

Here's to the maiden of bashful fifteen;
Here's to the widow of fifty;
Here's to the flaunting extravagant quean,
And here's to the housewife that's thrifty.
The School for Scandal
—Richard Brinsley Sheridan

I LEFT SOON after, but I didn't go back to town. I pulled off the road into a stand of chestnut trees, making sure I couldn't be seen from the highway, and slept in the car.

A little after midnight a chill wind woke me up. I turned on the radio and picked up police calls between the Peony Springs constable, Beauregard Stubb, and some members of the state militia.

"I'm still at the jail cells across from the courthouse." I recognized Beau's voice, though it sounded a little slurred. I wondered if he had been sampling Nick's white lightning. "The two MacKay boys are still here. I'm afraid if I leave, their kin will bust 'em out. Uhh, over."

"So who's going to come out here and take these folk into custody, Stubb? Over," said a voice I didn't recognize.

"Aren't there enough militia to send a detail back here with the ones you put under arrest? Over."

"Naw. We've cordoned off a huge section of the woods and it's going to take hours to look for evidence. Over."

"What do you think you're going to find in the dark? Why don't you just leave the markers in place and come back to town. Over."

"I guess you're right. Me and the men will come on into town. The boys can camp out for the night in the courthouse hallways. I'll get a room at the hotel."

I listened for another half hour and pieced together the story. Seems the Klan had come into town to finish some business with a certain party, and there had been too many for the constable on duty to stop them. The state militia had come to break up the Klan rally, but not without a fracas and a dozen casualties.

I TOOK MY time driving back. By the time I got to the woods and found the clearing the bonfire had died down. No one left but a body a-hanging.

I decided to pay my respects to the Widow DeCosta the next day.

A woman in mourning needed someone to lean upon.

JACKIE SUE

It is better to dwell in a corner of the housetop,
than with a brawling woman in a wide house.
— *Proverbs 21:9*

BRANT RANDALL

I.

"JACKIE SUE, ARE you ready?"

"Not yet, Ma. This curling iron ain't working like it used to."

I should have kept my mouth shut, because the next second my mother comes busting through the door.

"You are not curling your hair, young lady. This is a trial, not a social."

I was standing there in a half-slip and brassiere. I jerked a towel off the sink and covered my bosoms, embarrassed-like, striking a pose like that It-Girl, Clara Bow.

"Mother! Haven't you ever heard of knocking?" My voice went up a semitone, letting her know I was ready to get into it. "I'm nearly naked. What if my brothers saw me?"

"Don't take that tone with me. And don't try changing the subject. You put that curling iron down this instant."

"I can't go out in public with only half my hair curled."

She yanked the iron out of my hand. Her lips were pinched together so tight I think she could have cracked a brazil nut.

"You have five minutes to get yourself into the car, little miss. Get moving."

I took it real slow going out the bathroom door.

"Or what?" I said. "You going to leave without me? Don't forget I'm the one that's been called as a witness. It doesn't matter if you and Daddy are there at all, that's what the marshal said."

"We will be there with you, to shield you," said Ma, grabbing my arm. "We are not going to let our daughter be made into a spectacle for the rude entertainment of the town."

I jerked away and slammed my bedroom door in her face. "I don't have time to talk. I only have five minutes to get dressed, remember?"

I tried on several blouses before settling on a nice pink seersucker that showed my figure to some advantage. Plus I had a cloche hat that went with it just perfect. It wasn't more than a quarter of an hour before I presented myself on the porch. My father took one look, said "Oh lord," and hung his head.

Mother grabbed me by the back of the neck and jerked my ear to her mouth.

"You button up the top of your blouse. All the way. I won't have you shame this family any more than you already have. Now get in the car."

Ma threw herself into the front seat. I just stood by the rear door of our Chevrolet sedan and waited.

"What now?" screamed Ma.

"I thought you were teaching my brothers etiquette. I guess there's no gentlemen to open the door for me."

This was too much for Daddy. He gave me a stern look and roared, "Get in. Now."

I pushed Kyle aside as I slid onto the bench seat.

Kyle was only ten, but he had a smart mouth on him. "I may not be a gentleman," he said, sotto voce, "but you sure ain't no lady. Dicky's sister said you're just a common whore."

I smacked him across the face for that, and he let out a yelp, and Ma reached back from the front seat and yanked my bangs. That set Albert to crying. Course he's only six, but he's got a pair of lungs. My father scrunched up his face and looked straight ahead, like he couldn't hear nothing.

We thumped along the rutted road into town, settling down some as we passed people walking towards the courthouse. My ma was so mad she had those little white spots on her cheeks, you know what I mean? Me and Kyle ceased our bickering long enough to laugh about that.

It's a hoot getting Ma worked up like that.

II.

Doubt is the key to all knowledge.
— *Arabian Proverb*

IT AIN'T EASY being thirteen in this dump of a town. We don't have a roller rink or a movie theater. If it hadn't been for my grandma and grandpa taking us kids to the next town every month or so, I never would have seen a movie. And that would be a pure misery.

There's no restaurant other than Gladys' diner, and for some reason Ma won't let us eat there. The town square has a little bandstand, but they never play any jazz there, nothing but some crusty old veterans' oom-pah band.

Even if they had some decent music, there'd be no dancing, no siree. None of that sinful carrying on, not with the Baptists being as thick in this town as fleas on a dog. I heard once that the Baptists don't believe in having the sexual intercourse while standing up, 'cause it might lead to dancing.

There's nothing to do but go to school, and that's a snore. Back when I didn't know any better I was a regular whiz in class, getting straight A's. All that led to was them giving me harder work to do and more of it. I'm smarter than that. I learned to do just enough to get by with C's and B's.

I mean, what good would it do me to be the high school valedictorian in this one-horse town? The only jobs for a woman here are clerking, waitressing, and taking in laundry.

Come the weekend I have to do chores all day Saturday, then sit through two services on Sunday. You'd think the church elders could at least find a preacher with some personality instead of that old fart, Dr. Summerfield.

And the Sunday School class. Miss Hicks looks like she might have been Methuzaleh's grandma, teaching those same old wheezes to Ham, Shem, and Japheth.

I mean, stories about a boatload of every kind of animal in creation floating around for forty days and forty nights. What kept the lions from eating the lambs, or the robins from eating the worms?

And how did just eight people shovel all that manure? When the circus train came through town last summer I saw the mountain of poop they had to get rid of every day.

The whole thing just doesn't ring true. Praying to an invisible giant who's going to grant your wishes. And if you don't fess up to what you've done wrong, you're going to burn in a lake of fire. Whoever heard of a lake of fire? If it's a lake, it's full of water. And if it's full of water, it sure ain't on fire.

The way church folk carry on about things. Just thinking about something is a sin. I mean, what on earth is lusting in your heart?

Not that the boys don't lust after me. Now that my breasts have come full, I notice looks from most of the boys whose voices have broken. And a couple of the church elders as well.

Boys my age will do most anything I say just for a chance to touch them. And I'm only talking about touching them through my clothes. Anything else is just too dangerous.

One time me and Harold were playing hooky from Sunday School. Miss Hicks had been carrying on about the Gadarene swine and I'd had my fill of pig talk, so I left for the bathroom and didn't come back. Harold followed a minute later. He had stolen a pack of his father's Camels and we were smoking and talking by the bank of the Euphrates.

He asked and asked and asked if he could just feel for himself how soft the skin was on my bosom. He was so earnest I let him slip his finger inside my middy blouse.

No sooner had his finger brushed my breast than his face turned red and he began to stutter. I think he was trying to tell me that he loved me, but he was stuck saying "I luh, luh, luh, luh." Over and over, like a broken phonograph record. Finally he fell to his knees and began to froth at the mouth.

I hurried back inside and told Miss Hicks that Harold had been possessed by the devil. She rushed down to the riverbank followed by the entire Sunday School class and discovered Harold lying there, thrashing about. His eyes were rolled back in his head and he'd wet himself.

You can imagine my embarrassment.

But I guess I can't say church is all bad. It does give me a chance to meet boys from other schools, because I sure am tired of the ones that have been in every single class with me all through grade school.

It's important to meet new people. They broaden your horizons and give you a sense of what else is going on in the world. That Angus DeCosta gave me some ideas about how I might get out of this town and find me some excitement.

Of course, come to think of it, just meeting him had already brought me more excitement than I thought humanly possible in Peony Springs. The trial would be pure entertainment. It would make me the most famous girl in the county. Everybody would be talking about me.

I mean that positive. Not like when Amelia Pinkerton got herself in a family way and had to go live in Nebraska on her aunt and uncle's farm and slop hogs and do sundry chores until the baby was born. I heard they put the infant in an orphanage, and when Amelia came back to town she didn't return to high school. She just started working as clerk at the five and dime. I saw her just last week, and she didn't look happy.

Well, Amelia never was too smart and she was plain as a mud fence. Probably had to do it just to get any boy to pay attention to her at all. Still, in this day and age you'd think she'd have used a French letter.

Some girls.

III.

Conscience is as good as a thousand witnesses.
— *Italian Proverb*

THE BAILIFF TOLD my parents they would have to sit in the visitor's gallery, upstairs in the heat. He took me to sit in a small room on a bench, next to some other townies that they were going to call as witnesses.

"You are not to discuss the case amongst yourselves," he said to all of us.

I raised my hand, feeling like this was official court business.

"Are these all the witnesses, sir?"

"You don't have to raise your hand, Miss. This isn't school," he said.

I didn't see why he had to be mean to me. I could see he was staring at my chest, so I crossed my arms in defense, making sure everyone noticed what he was doing. "Well, are they?" I said. "I mean, where's Angus DeCosta?"

One of the men cursed under his breath. All I caught was "little piece of spit."

The bailiff pinned the man with a look. "DeCosta's already in the dock. He's the first to testify."

I liked the word testify. It sounded important, like we'd be doing something that would change the world.

I leaned back, satisfied. The bailiff gave us all one more warning look and left the room.

Mrs. Harmon was there, the old biddy. She was looking daggers at me, though I hardly knew her. I looked daggers right back at her. It's just awful how jealous an old woman gets once she's lost her looks. Not that she ever could have had that much to brag about, but now with her tits hanging down to her waist, and her crazy hair, she was a caution.

I inspected the rest of the witnesses. I recollected some of them from the picnic, but I was certain others had not been there when my cousins first came upon me and Angus.

I pointed to one of the men I didn't recall. "Why are you here? You weren't at the church social. What can you possibly testify about?"

He looked at me for a long moment. "We aren't s'pose to discuss the case, are we? That's what he said, wasn't it?"

"Who's talking about the case? I'm trying to figure out what you can tell them when you weren't at the church social."

He thought that over a moment.

"I was on the bridge when they threw that DeCosta kid off. That's what I can tell them about. How it wasn't attempted murder a-tall. It was strictly trying to protect a woman's honor." He looked me right in the eye. "Protect *your* honor. Though I'm not so sure you have any."

I couldn't sit still for that kind of vicious slander. I jumped up and slapped him across the face.

"You better keep a civil tongue. My daddy'll…"

He cut me off by slapping me back. That brought two

more men off the bench, each grabbing one of us. Mrs. Harmon set up a screech that sounded like a fire alarm.

In five seconds the bailiff was back, a wild look in his eye.

It took some minutes before things were calm again. The bailiff decided maybe I should have a little room all to myself.

"What am I supposed to do in here alone?" I said.

He sighed, ducked into the hall, and was back about thirty seconds later. He handed me several magazines.

"Read these. Improve your mind."

"There's no call to be rude," I said.

"Wasn't for you, the county wouldn't be wasting tax-payer dollars on a trial."

"Wasn't for trials the taxpayers wouldn't have to waste money on your salary, either."

His mouth puckered like he'd bit into something sour. He slammed the door on his way out.

I looked through the magazines. *Trial Lawyer. Journal of Jurisprudence. Association of County Governments.* I would have been better off with the King James. Least a few of those stories have some action.

I took out the compact I had sneaked from Ma's dresser and freshened up what little makeup I was allowed to wear. I couldn't get a satisfactory view of how I looked after my tussle in the other room, so I poked my head out the door. The coast was clear and I went to find the ladies' room.

I ran into the marshal's dog in the corridor. He came up and pushed his nose into my privates the way dogs do. Put me in mind of something I heard my daddy say, how there were too many boys sniffing round me these days.

Boys and hounds do have some similarities, I suppose. They both like getting too close and personal right away. But they're easy to distract if you give them some little tidbit.

"How you doing today, Chief? You being a good doggie? You guarding the courthouse 'cause it's so full of folks you don't know?"

Chief stared into my eyes like he was trying to understand, and let his tongue droop out of the side of his mouth. He looked at my small purse as if he suspected there might be something to eat inside it. Made me laugh and it made him drool.

Anyway I gave Chief a good scratch behind the ears, he sniffed deep a couple more times, then let out a satisfied *whuff.*

Once in the bathroom the mirror showed me there was damage to repair, and I spent the next twenty minutes redoing my makeup, straightening my clothes, and setting that hat just right to let one little curl peek out.

A woman I didn't know came in, all business. She had a nice pencil skirt and silk blouse, hair cut like Claudette Colbert. She was carrying a notebook. As she washed her hands she caught my eye in the mirror.

"He's quite the handsome dog, isn't he?"

"You mean Chief?"

She gave me a funny look. "I meant Angus DeCosta. Half the women in the courtroom are swooning over him. Not that he seemed to take any notice of them. He acted like all that attention was the most natural thing in the world."

"Is he still testifying? Maybe I can take a gander."

"He just finished. The bailiff led him off somewhere. He caused too much ruckus among the folks in the gallery to let him to stay in the courtroom."

She left and I began to think about what I would say as I was testifying in court. I unfastened the top button of my blouse.

Two hours and four more trips to the bathroom later I was finally called to the witness stand.

IV.

Through all the lying days of my youth,
I swayed my leaves and flowers in the sun.
The Coming of Wisdom with Time
— William Butler Yeats

THE BAILIFF PLACED me in this little cubby next to the judge's tall desk. They call it the witness box. Every eye was on me and I felt like I was a film star or something. Which sits just fine with my own future plans.

I caught sight of the woman I had met in the bathroom, taking notes on a pad of paper. She was sitting in the front row, right behind Andrew and Angus MacKay.

There was a man unknown to me sitting next to my cousins. He was maybe thirty or so, not bad looking for a man of his age. I guessed he was their lawyer.

The judge looked over the end of his nose and right down my blouse. He gave a little smile to himself and motioned to the bailiff.

A Bible was placed in front of me.

"Place your right hand on the Bible, raise your left hand, and repeat after me," said the bailiff.

"I'm left-handed," I said. "Does that make any difference?" I gave an innocent look, the kind Mary Pickford is so good at.

The spectators in the courtroom laughed out loud at

that, causing Judge Halbertson to rap his gavel several times and demand order.

"Which hand you use is not germane, Miss Palmer," said the judge.

"Of course it's not German," said I. "I'm an American, born right here in Potemkin County."

That drew another round of guffaws from the gallery.

I saw this was going to be a good crowd.

The bailiff glared at the citizens who were laughing. I thought the judge might break either his gavel or the top of his desk. I put my eyes down and looked demure. At least I think I did. I was trying to.

The bailiff placed my left hand on the Bible. "Do you solemnly swear to tell…"

"I most certainly do not swear. My parents raised me to be ladylike."

I smiled at my mother and father in the gallery, and most of the courtroom turned to look at them. My mother first turned red, then went pale. My father dropped his head into his hands. My two brothers waved at me, and I gave a little wave back.

Judge Halbertson slammed his gavel down right next to me, and I gave a little jump, registering surprise with a hand to my heart, the way Zasu Pitts does.

"Young lady, this is a court of law, and the law is not to be mocked. If you cause any more commotion I will charge you with contempt of court."

I saw that this part of my act was finished.

"I'm sorry," I said, with pretty good contrition. "I've never been in a court before. I'm only thirteen, your honor."

The judge and bailiff both looked down my blouse this

time, while the judge mouthed "Thirteen?" to himself.

Course I'll be fourteen next week.

We got through the swearing-in stuff, and identifying myself for the record, then a bunch of boring questions from Prosecutor Sykes about my family relationships and my education and, at last, my whereabouts on the 28th of August.

"So you were at a social gathering sponsored by a church. Which church was that?"

"The Union Methodist. But it was the annual all-church do, so all the other churches were there, too. The Presbyterians, Episcopalians, Church of Christ, Lutherans." I smiled. "Even the Baptists, bless their hearts."

This got a big laugh. Sykes repeated, "'Bless their hearts.' Is that so?"

"That's how Reverend Summerfield puts it. He says the Baptists are sincere, but a little backward. It's up to the real Christians to help them along life's difficult path, make sure they get through the pearly gates."

This drew another laugh from everyone in the room, except the Baptists. They looked askance at their neighbors, not having realized before now that their intellect had been called into question from the pulpit.

I felt my testimony was going strong.

"Is this to some purpose, counselor?" said Judge Halbertson, after gaveling the room to order. "This isn't going to become a theological debate, is it?"

Sykes pretended to look chastened, like the judge had cut off his best argument. "No, sir." He shuffled through his notes. "We have heard from Angus DeCosta that he was sharing a dish of ice cream with you."

"Yes. Strawberry."

The Judge gave a grumpy little snort and looked at me.

"Only answer Mr. Sykes' direct question. Don't volunteer irrelevant information."

"I just thought it might be important, your honor." I gave him a sweet smile, showing how helpful I was trying to be.

Sykes continued. "The two of you chose to take the dish of ice cream away from the other children of your age?"

I bristled at that 'children' remark, but held my tongue.

"He said that you sought the shade of a large rhododron," Sykes went on.

"It was very hot. We hoped the shade would keep the ice cream from melting so fast."

"Andrew MacKay testified that you and Angus DeCosta had hidden yourselves among the branches of the bush and that you couldn't be seen by the other children."

"Like I said, we were trying to find some deep shade to protect our ice cream." This children business was beginning to burn me up. "And besides, if we were so hidden, how did Andrew and his brother just walk right up to us?" I said with some heat.

"Just answer his question, Miss Palmer," butted in the judge.

I gave him a look. "I didn't hear any question, just a bunch of malarkey about rhododendrons."

The judge rolled his eyes and nodded to Mr. Sykes.

"Had you ever met the DeCosta boy before that day?"

"No, but then I hadn't met plenty of the *boys* that were at the picnic. They came from churches all over the county."

"And yet you felt safe with him when you were hiding in the bushes?"

What the heck was he getting at?

I guess I had felt safe enough with Angus, but it also felt plenty dangerous at the same time. He was one smooth talker, handsome as the devil, and had what we girls call a manly physique. I had known at the time we were going to get into some mischief. Still, remembering what the judge had said concerning irrelevant information, I gave my best innocent look and nodded.

"Yes, I guess so."

"When your cousins, Angus and Andrew MacKay, came upon the two of you, what followed?"

I certainly wasn't going to talk about where I had my hands and where he had his. I decided to stick with all the truth that was fit to be repeated in public.

"My cousins didn't like me being with a boy they didn't know. They're protective of me about such things. Overly protective, I'd say."

I didn't add that they have each been giving me the eye since last Christmas.

"Protective in what way?"

"Angus reached right over and grabbed Angus by the ear."

Judge Halbertson stuck his oar in. "Well, first we have one Angus and now we have another. We'll have to refer to this as the case of the two An-guy." He beamed a toothy smile around the room to let everyone know this was humor.

No one seemed to get it, except the prosecutor and the public defender who each chuckled in a half-hearted way. I guess being on the public payroll does that to you; you have to laugh at the big shot's jokes.

"They commenced to calling each other names, my cousin twisted DeCosta's ear, and got a bite taken out of his leg in exchange," I said. "Meantime Andrew jerked me out of the bush and began yelling to the adults that something bad had happened."

"And what did he say had happened?" said Mr. Sykes.

"I don't like to say. It's embarrassing and it isn't true."

"You're required to answer, Miss Palmer," said Halbertson.

Don't judges have any sense of decency?

"He told them I had been—well, interfered with. The church ladies gathered around and hustled me away, though I told them nothing had happened."

Strictly speaking, this was true, even though we had been playing a little peek-a-boo with our privates. I didn't think that needed to be mentioned.

"And what happened to Mister DeCosta?"

"I don't know. I couldn't see anything else, surrounded as I was by the women. I just heard yelling and lots of commotion, then DeCosta was tossed into a pickup truck and they all drove off."

Sykes took his seat, and I felt that I had showed myself to good advantage. I rose from the witness box, but the bailiff motioned that I should stay seated.

My cousins' attorney came over to the witness box. He didn't appear to be either a happy person or well disposed towards me. This proved to be true.

"Isn't it true, Miss Palmer, that when my clients found you with Mr. DeCosta, he had his hands inside your clothing?"

The audience gave a little gasp at that. I fear I turned somewhat red.

"No," I said, low and angry.

"I'm sorry, Miss Palmer, could you please speak up so that the court may hear you? Are you denying that he had his hands under your shirt when you were discovered?"

I pursed my lips. "I already said no."

"Remember that you are under oath, Miss Palmer."

I might have been "under oath," but I am not under-equipped with sense.

"Yes," I said.

"Yes, you admit that his hands were—"

"Yes, I remember that I am under oath."

I was also under a roof, but what of it?

"We have previous testimony that your hands were inside Mr. DeCosta's trousers."

I was steaming now. "That's a lie. Do I look like the kind of girl who would carry on like that?"

Somebody from the balcony hollered, "Boy, howdy!"

I swiveled to face the gallery, looking for whoever called that out. I saw the culprit, grinning like an idjit. I jumped to my feet and pointed him out to the crowd.

"Bobby Fate, you are in contempt of court!"

I guess the rest of the spectators found this funny, because the laughter was long and raucous. The judge gaveled until his hand was sore.

"Bailiff, you will remove that person from the court-room," he said, pointing to Bobby. He paused to let his angry glare sweep across the rest of the spectators. "And I won't hesitate to eject any of you, excepting you act with decorum in my court."

My interrogation resumed and it went on for some time, with plenty of rude questions. No matter what I said, the attorney twisted it around like I was some kind of tramp and my cousins had been protecting the family reputation. The prosecutor objected from time to time, and once the two attorneys got together at the other side of the judge's desk and talked in whispers.

I took the opportunity to look around the courtoom. The heat had the spectators fanning themselves. I saw my youngest brother had fallen asleep. My parents' faces seemed to have turned to stone, and I noticed that the people sitting next to them had pulled away some little distance.

The judge slapped his hand on the desktop and the legal huddle broke up. The prosecutor went back to his table, looking unsettled.

The defense lawyer came after me again. He leaned into the witness box, right in my face, and pointed his finger at me.

"Miss Palmer, I understand that this isn't the first young man you have been seen with, behaving in an unbecoming manner."

I drew back and put my hand to my throat. I looked at the judge for help.

"Your honor, did you see how he looked into my blouse? I believe this man is sex obsessed, the way he carries on."

That pretty much brought down the house. The judge gaveled some more, the prosecutor smiled, and soon I was let out of the witness box. As I looked around the court I realized that this town was pretty well played out for me.

The bailiff took my elbow to escort me back to my little room.

"I want to watch the rest of the testimony," I said.

The bailiff swept me out the door. "His honor feels you are a disruptive influence in the courtroom." He opened the door to my closet. "You are to stay here in case you need to be recalled for further testimony."

"How come I didn't see Mr. DeCosta in there?"

The bailiff grimaced. "He was disruptive, too."

I gave him a look. "What about lunch? I'm getting hungry."

"When there is a lunch recess, something will be brought to you. We get our comestibles from Gladys' diner."

"I've never tasted the food from there. Is it any good?"

He just sniffed and closed the door.

V.

It is a bad plan that admits of no modification.
— *Publilius Syrus*

I WAITED FIVE minutes, then made a break for the bathroom. I nosed along the halls, looking into the various rooms. It didn't take long to find Angus. I stayed out in the hall and talked with him through the partly open door. I figured if the bailiff came back I could claim I was lost. It would have been hard to explain actually being in the room with DeCosta.

"Angus, you still owe me three dollars."

Angus gave a forced smile. His leg was in a cast and he had it propped up on a chair. His crutches were standing against the wall. He looked like he was in pain.

"Yeah, well," was all he said.

"I mean fair is fair. You said you'd give me three dollars if I showed you my possum."

A look of consternation passed over his face. "You didn't tell the court about that, did you?"

"I wasn't born yesterday," I said.

He looked relieved. "Say, I showed you my squirrel. I think we're even."

I was getting impatient. "I hope they recall me to the stand this afternoon. I've remembered some details I forgot to mention the first time."

He looked alarmed, which I found delightful. He was extra cute with a little fear on his face.

He shrugged and pulled a wallet from his hip pocket. I let him extract three singles and fold them up. As he was about to toss them to me, I stopped him.

"I don't need your money, Angus. I need your help."

Angus looked wary as he put the dollars away. "Help for what?"

"I want out of this town in the worst way. My reputation is ruined here. Thanks to you, I might add."

He didn't say anything, just waited for the penny to drop.

"I need about thirty dollars rail fare to Hollywood, maybe another ten for food along the way, say ten for a week's rental of a room with board while I find work as an actress."

"You must be crazy if you think I have fifty bucks."

"What about your father?"

"Most likely he's going to be in jail for a while."

"Okay, then your mother."

Angus squirmed around for a bit, looking for a more comfortable position.

"She doesn't have it, either." He hesitated, then blurted out. "She just bailed me out of a difficult spot with a girl in another town. She's skinned."

I mulled that over and a new idea came to me. "You suppose you have some friends be willing to pay three dollars to see my possum?"

"Shoot, some of them would probably pay five." He looked me over. "Even more if you let them, you know, do it."

I shook my head. "No. I may need that currency in

Hollywood. Strictly a look is all they get. A good look, say a full minute."

I thought that I didn't want my past catching up to me once I was a star. I put on a Louise Brooks pout.

"And they're not going to see my face. I've got an idea for a little stage in a room. You'll have to act as bouncer and bodyguard. I wouldn't want to cry rape, now would I?"

"You're a wonder, that's for sure." He looked doubtful. "Seems like a lot of trouble and risk."

"You just get hold of thirty of your dirty-minded friends in one day, especially the under fourteens. Fast talker like you will set it up in no time. I'll let you keep all the take above the fifty dollars I require."

He just stared, calculating his end. "When?"

"I'm talking two days after this trial is over and you're back in your own town."

His mouth dropped open. I closed the door.

Back in my little room I thought my plan through in more detail. It seemed solid. The way he had taken the bait told me I was onto something. Males just don't have good judgment when it comes to this kind of thing.

Personally, I don't see the big attraction. Granny MacKay gave me a silver-plated brush, comb, and hand mirror last Christmas. With the hand mirror I've spent some time inspecting the possum and there just isn't much to it.

Still, boys'll be boys.

Hollywood, here I come.

EBENEEZER KAUZ

It ain't what you don't know
that gets you into trouble.
It's what you know for sure
that just ain't so.
— *Mark Twain*

I.

"THIS PLACE HAS gone to hell, Gladys."

I was the only customer in the diner, but even so, Gladys didn't bother looking at me. She finished cutting up the chicken, setting the pieces aside while she mixed flour, pepper, and some fine-chopped lemon rind. I could smell the lemon from where I sat.

"What's stuck in your craw today, Eben?"

I waved the newspaper at her.

"You see this?"

She glanced at the headline, went back to dredging chicken in the flour mix.

"Well, it's big news, ain't it? Attempted murders, savage attacks, a girl interfered with and all." She rolled her lazy eye my direction. "You don't expect the editor to skip all that, do you?"

"I'm not talking about that salacious tripe. That's not news anyway. That's just scandal. Folks ought to keep shet about it."

I realized I was losing the train of my argument. I pointed to the price of the paper.

"They raised the price to a nickel," I said. "And it's just a rural county rag, not a real newspaper at all."

"No one's making you read it."

"That's not the point. Last week's edition cost three cents. This one's five cents, but it's the same number of pages as last week. Nor do I see sixty-seven percent improvement in the contents."

"Don't get yourself worked up. A man your age ought to spend his energy on more important things."

"What more important things? Inflation's going to ruin the entire country, and this small-time-journalist-jumped-up-editor thinks he ought to raise his price by two thirds."

I tried to give her a dirty look, but she wasn't paying attention. "A man my age, indeed," I said to myself.

Gladys put a big spoonful of bacon grease on the griddle, where it sizzled, filling the room with its aroma. She looked over at me, took the paper and examined the front page.

"Sixty-seven per cent, my left foot. You didn't pay nuthin for this, Ebeneezer Kauz. Marshal Lawe left this paper behind, after he et his breakfast special. Your so-called price increase is two-thirds of zero."

"It's the principle of the thing, consarn it."

I hated losing the point and I tried to cover my discomfort by taking a sip of coffee, but my cup was dry. I held it up to her. She sighed, but poured me another cup, looking aggravated.

"I s'pose you're going to start charging for refills," I said.

"That's your sixth cup, Uncle."

Gladys may be my grandniece on my mother's side, but I had never met the girl until I fetched up in this little hole of a town in the mountains. When she called me Uncle, I knew I had crossed a line.

"I paid my nickel, just like everybody else. Got my doughnut and cuppa joe. Says free refills right on the menu."

"Everybody else doesn't sit here half the day drinking up my profits, Uncle."

"I don't want charity, even if you are kin. All I want is what I paid for, like it says in black and white. I remember when coffee and a doughnut wasn't but two cents."

I must have raised my voice some because the Negro dishwasher came out from the back room and gave me a look. Gladys motioned to him that things were okay, but he continued to stand there, glaring at me.

"Darnell, there's no reason to be giving him the evil eye," said Gladys.

I heard him mutter something about white devils. Colored man oughtn't talk like that if he knows what's good for him.

"You don't know what you're talking about, boy," I said.

I guess being called boy didn't sit too well with him, because he came around the counter. He probably figured he could get away with that, me being eighty-one years old and all.

"It's time for you to get on outside, old man."

Gladys got in between the two of us. "You two stop right where you are." Her face flushed with anger. "Darnell, I want to introduce you to my granduncle, Ebeneezer Kauz."

From the way Darnell's mouth dropped open I surmised he was as surprised as I was. Gladys seemed to enjoy our consternation.

"And Uncle Eben, I want you meet my cousin from Virginia, Darnell Boggs."

"You say this bit of midnight is your cousin?"

"Darnell's the son of my mother's sister-in-law, Tanessa."

All three of us chewed that over for a while.

"That sort of makes Darnell my grandnephew-in-law, the way I calculate it," I said.

Darnell said, "Yeah, well the way I calc'late it, you're still a rude ol' geezer."

He kind of smiled, so I did too, showing him all seven of my teeth.

"You two got that out of your system now?" said Gladys. "You going to behave?"

Darnell went back behind the counter. I knew I'd been difficult and it had been my boisterous voice that had started the trouble, but I didn't see why I had to roll over like some puppy.

"Gladys, if you're so set on passing for white, why'd you bring the dark side of your family into the diner?"

She gave me a look. "Get off your high horse, Uncle. You've been passing for sixty years the way I heard it told."

"You ought to ask before you start telling my business, missy," I said.

That got Darnell's attention.

"Mean to say you're...?"

I saw there was nothing for it but to explain somewhat to this new relation of mine.

"Three of my grandparents was white. It was my mother's dad that was half Negro, half light-skinned Cherokee. Why, I remember the time that—"

Darnell shook his head, gave me a condescending look. "Injun, huh?"

It's been my experience that all these newcomers to America—and by that I mean the Dutch, the French, the English, the Spaniards, the Germans, and what all—all of them look down on the black man. Ain't nobody left for the black man to look down upon 'cept the Indian, and he can only do that because the Indians was so weak they let the newcomers take their land away.

Made me want to wipe that look off his face.

"What are you, Darnell? Thirty, thirty-two?"

He nodded assent, looked wary.

"How long were you a yard bird?" I looked him over, saw the ropy muscles, thick calluses. "Or was it chain gang?"

His eyes sparked a moment, but he held his tongue. I started toward the door.

"Yeah, that's right. It still shows," I said over my shoulder. "Your cousin's going out on a limb for you, Darnell. Don't disappoint her." I took a breath. "I'm going to go talk to that so-called editor."

I stepped out into the autumn sunshine. The brightness made me blink and I forgot for a moment where I was going.

II.

I would sooner be honestly damned
than hypocritically immortalized.
— *Davy Crockett*

LIKE I SAID, I'm eighty-one and damn glad to be this old. I tell my age to every single soul that seems to show an interest and to many who don't.

Anyone who can cipher knows that I was born in 1847. What they don't know is that I grew up among the Eastern Band Cherokee in North Carolina, since my mama favored her daddy. She got both his Cherokee features and his kinky hair.

It was 1846 when a German drummer of farm implements left her pregnant, though she was but sixteen. I got his fair skin and gray eyes, but not his name, since he shunned my mother once she told him she was with child.

Times was hard on my grandparents' mountain farm. Still, my mother and I were reasonably happy there, at least up to the point my grandparents died.

After that it was just too much for one woman to do, raising a boy, trying to keep the livestock from starving, keeping us clothed and fed. Mama got thinner and thinner, with a hard light shining from behind her eyes.

By the time I was fifteen, it felt as if I was drowning. I wanted to see more of the world than just another mountainside in the Smokies. I could read some, and what I read made me want to see the rest of the county, both the Carolinas, the whole blamed United States.

When the War of Secession broke out I saw my chance to get off the farm and earn a steady paycheck. It seemed to me I'd be doing a good thing, something to lighten Mama's load.

When she heard I wanted to enlist, I found out otherwise.

"So you're going to leave home for the glories of war." She grabbed my arm and looked me full in the face. "I didn't realize I'd birthed a fool."

I had feared that she might come after me for undertaking such a dangerous course. I thought I had the reply to distract her.

"Surely my wages will make things easier for you, Mama. You needn't work so hard."

"Don't give me that drivel. That's not why you're going."

She always could see through me.

"Do you know what you'd be fighting for?" she said.

"The Carolinas have the right to determine their own destiny. If we want to leave the Union, we can."

She gave me a hard look, then sat down at our deal table. She pulled the lamp close to her.

"Look at my face, Ebeneezer. You can see Cherokee blood, my Negro blood. The men with whom you will eat and sleep, the men you will fight beside don't believe I'm a human being. Men like them *owned* your grandfather. They'd own me if they could, just for the way I look."

"This is a matter of states rights. Slavery doesn't figure into it."

She gave me a look of disbelief.

"The only protection I have is the remoteness of these mountains and my Cherokee neighbors, and that protection is mighty thin," she said. "Now you want to be part of taking even that little bit away."

"None of the men I met owned slaves, nor wanted to." I was anxious to persuade her I was doing the right thing. "You're seeing this through old eyes, Mama. These are new times."

She pulled away from me. I couldn't tell whether she was hurt or disgusted.

"Answer me this, Ebeneezer Screech Owl. Did you enlist using your real name?"

"Mama, even the other Cherokee have stopped using the old names."

"Answer the question."

My father being German, I'd decided to use his language.

"I'm Private Kauz."

She slapped me across the face and cursed me so hard I didn't take time to pack. I left right then, walked all night into town, and was waiting by the recruiting station door at sunrise.

I wrote to her from the front line after the first Battle of Manassas, but she never wrote back.

She didn't last the winter.

III.

It is only those who have neither fired a shot,
nor heard the shrieks and groans
of the wounded, who cry aloud for blood...
War is hell.
— *William Tecumseh Sherman*

CHIEF WAS STRETCHED out in the shade near the jail. I went over, squatted down, and gave his head and shoulders a good rub. It always pays to be friendly to police dogs.

"Chief, you be a good dog. Only bite the bad guys, yes?"

Chief didn't seem to follow my reasoning, just let his tongue hang out and panted. It took more effort than I foresaw to stand up straight again, and I broke a light sweat. All that coffee was doing me harm. I'd have to watch my diet.

"Mornin', Eben."

I turned and saw Lars Gunnarsen, our town's only full-time drunk, standing in the alley. I noted the paper sack in his hand, and I have to say I licked my lips.

"You're up early, Lars," I said, though it was some time after eleven.

Lars waved me over.

During the sixty years since the end of the war, I've

taken many a beating when people find out I wore the rebel gray. I've no one to tell my tales of the war now that I live in the North. No one except Lars. That's the basis of our friendship.

Lars is a veteran of the Spanish American War, left his right arm in Cuba. It's my guess that he did other things in Cuba he'd rather forget, hence his thirty year sojourn at the bottom of the bottle.

"I ever tell you about the Battle of El Caney, Eben?" said Lars.

"Every time I see you. But if you give me a sip from whatever's in that bag, I believe I could enjoy the story yet again."

This being our standard greeting, we cackled like jays.

So Lars began his recollection about how he won the battle single-handed. Somewhere along the line we both took a seat on the ground, backs against the alley wall, our legs sticking out in front of us. I sipped and nodded and oh-my'ed until he rambled to a halt. Then I passed him the bottle and told him about the Battle of Second Manassas.

As I recounted it, I began to relive it.

"We fought until nearly midnight the first day. It was after the guns stopped that I could hear them."

Lars was busy taking a big pull. As he swallowed he lost track of what I was saying.

"Hear them? Hear who?"

"The soldiers. The wounded. The men lying in the dirt that first night, crying for their mothers, screaming in pain, begging for water, praying aloud for death to take them."

"What soldiers were those?"

"Didn't matter. There were both blue and gray a-lying out there, almost two thousand dead that day alone. Another five thousand wounded. When those men died they shit their britches, and the stench was something powerful. If there's anything closer to being in Hell while still living, I don't want to know about it."

"Yeah, I 'member that," said Lars.

"What are you talking about? You weren't even born yet."

"Naw, I mean the same thing happened at El Caney."

"No, it didn't. This was fighting under General Wheeler."

"That's right. I was fighting under Wheeler at El Caney."

"Can't be," I said. "He was a Confederate general."

"Well, the Republic re-commissioned him for the Spanish American War, and he ordered the charges at El Caney. He hadn't learned a thing. Same damn formations he'd used during the Civil War."

I cut him off.

"No more talk of El Caney. S'my turn."

I reached for the bottle, only to find it was empty. I shook the bag and bottle at Lars, but he had fallen asleep.

I leaned back against the wall. I didn't want to sleep. I was afraid I might dream I was back in Manassas.

The nightmares were not as bad since the Great War in Europe. Reading the accounts of the bloodbaths of trench warfare in Europe had served to ease the memories of the great slaughters the Union and the Confederacy exacted upon each other.

My bladder ain't what it used to be. The 'shine and six cups of coffee were crying out for discharge. I considered relieving myself on Lars' shoes, since I always enjoyed a good practical joke, but thought better of it. I wanted to enjoy the hospitality of his bottle another day. I pulled myself up the brick wall and made my way behind the building.

I had just finished doing my business—and at my age that's an accomplishment—when I saw Jedediah Spout make his way to the rear of Gladys' diner, knocking at the back door.

Jedediah looked to be surprised when Darnell came out, but they exchanged a few words I couldn't hear. I sidled closer, keeping to the dark shade against the wall. When Gladys came out to speak to Jedediah I could make out some of what was said.

What I heard didn't make much sense. What did the head of the Klan have to do with Bill Sykes? And why on earth was Gladys helping to pass along a note? They finished jawing and Gladys went back inside. Spout took off into the brush toward the creek.

I thought it over. There was a mystery here and I wanted to solve it. I straightened my clothes, then circled back to the front of the diner and went inside.

"Gladys! I want to apologize for my rudeness earlier."

It looked as though Gladys might lose her dentures.

"Is there something I can do to make up for it?" I said.

Gladys looked me up and down. It's apparent this gal was born with a suspicious nature.

"You angling for a free lunch, Eben?"

I gave her a look to let her know she had insulted my integrity.

In the end she let me carry the gallon of punch to the

courthouse. She wrote Bill Sykes' name on the back of Spout's note and gave me instructions to have the bailiff hand it directly to Sykes.

I ambled across the street, taking a moment in the shade of the doorway to unfold the note and peruse it.

And that left me with another mystery. All it said was, *The men will be in town by 8:30.*

What men? And why were they coming to town? And why was the Kleagle of the local KKK confirming it with the Potemkin County prosecuting attorney? And was that eight-thirty tonight or tomorrow morning?

All I knew was that if that cracker Jedediah Spout was involved, it was bad news.

I couldn't get it to make any sense. I went on inside and sat down with the bailiff at the rear of the courtroom, passing him the re-folded note. He bustled over to the prosecutor's table and conferred with Big Bill Sykes, doing his best to look important in the eyes of the town folk.

The bailiff and I each had a Dixie cup of punch. It was tasty, but five minutes later my stomach was in rebellion. Too much acid in one morning.

I went in search of the facilities and run into a young filly, that Palmer girl who had stirred up the current situation. I'd heard she'd been molested, but seeing the way she was outfitted, I began to think otherwise. She was dressed like a whore in training and I thought her parents ought to give her a serious talking to.

She seemed startled to meet me in the halls of the courthouse, but tried to hide it. She pretended she was lost.

"Do you know where the ladies' room is, mister?"

"In eighty-one years I've never had occasion to use it, so I don't."

She gave me a sour look and flounced off. I heard her mention "fart" under her breath, but I wasn't sure if she were speaking of her own digestive problems or mine.

My stomach flip-flopped again and I quick-stepped down the hall.

I'm here to tell you I was sorry to see that doughnut go. It was the only food I had eaten since noon the day before.

I checked my pocket, though I already knew it held but fourteen cents. I wouldn't be buying lunch.

IV.

> It is not the man who has little,
> but the man who craves more,
> that is poor.
> — *Seneca*

THOUGH I HAVE great respect for the Roman poet Seneca, he neglected to mention my case: I had little, but I needed a little bit more.

I napped for a couple of hours, hoping to escape the heat of the day and maybe make my innards forget how empty they were. I woke up to hear my stomach growling as it tried to chew on itself. I was going to have come up with something to fill it.

When all is said and done, I am yet a mountain boy from the Smokies. I know how to fish and gather edibles in the forest. I went into the Confederate Army already knowing how to shoot. I supplied supper meat many a time to the men in my platoon. I still move pretty quiet through the forest, and I can hunt if I'm able to get close enough to see what I'm aiming at.

My little bachelor shack was a leftover from a mine that had closed. Wasn't no more than eight foot square, just room enough for bed, chair, table, and stove. The latter served to keep the place warm in winter. A nail by the door served as all the clothes rack I had need of. I generally had most of my clothes on my back at any particular time.

Outhouse wasn't too far off. No running water in the cabin, but a spring nearby yields a slow trickle that fills a bucket in a couple of hours. It's humble, but it's home.

I plucked down my cane fishing pole from its spot above the door, and got a hook from the coffee can on the windowsill. I went outside to dig a worm or three.

While I was delving, Lars came by, all in a lather.

"Eben, you missed out on the excitement."

"I don't think so, Lars. After all, I fought in this country's greatest war, I've worked on the Vanderbilt's railroad, I've—What was I talking about?"

"I said you missed the excitement."

"Yeah? What's that?"

"Marshal Lawe took that Nick DeCosta fella out of jail, walked him across to the courthouse."

I went back to digging for worms. Lars looked crestfallen that I didn't make a to-do over his news.

"That ain't all, Eben. Then Lawe and the court bailiff threw three of the McKays out of court."

"You don't say. Well, I'm not surprised. Those MacKays have always been a rowdy bunch. Say, did I ever tell you about the time that four of 'em—"

"Those boys were pretty angry," interrupted Lars. "They threatened to come back to town with more kin and cause a fuss."

"Lars, I don't mean to be rude, but I'm trying to get some bait. I've always found that earthworms and night crawlers work best. Course it's not night right now, so I'm not expecting to find any of those. I don't go for those fancy hand-tied flies and all. The point is, I want to get down to the creek and catch me some dinner."

Lars perked up at that.

"You get any bullhead or catfish, invite me over, okay?"

"I'd consider it if you bring along the sauce."

"The sauce?"

"I like a little corn sauce to help the fish slide down."

"Corn sauce?" Lars was befuddled. "Oh, you mean 'shine. I'll go over to Granny MacKay's and get us a bottle." He chuckled to himself. "A little corn sauce, eh?"

Now that he had a mission, he bobbed his head and set off in the approximate direction of the MacKay place. I took off in the opposite direction, heading for a crick that empties into the Euphrates.

It was still ten days until my railway pension check would arrive. I didn't see what I was going to do. It wasn't like I'd never been through a patch of difficulty. I'd always been able to pull through before, but my body betrays me now and again.

While I'd served in the Rebel Army I gained some knowledge of railways. As I saw the men and materiel shuttled from battle to battle, I realized the future lay in mechanical transportation. I made it my business to ask questions every time I rode the rails.

In April of 1865, when the end came for our cause, I chose not to surrender. Instead I faded back into the woods and made my way home. It was a perilous passage.

I looted clothes from the bodies of civilians. I filched food from farmers who themselves had not enough to feed their families.

I appropriated a mule from a Negro trying to get his

field planted, but it gave up the ghost two days later. Made me wish I had left it alone. Maybe that family would have got their seed into the ground.

When needs must, I rode shanks' mare. I reached the farmstead by summer to find my mother's grave unmarked and the buildings burned to the ground. I moped around for two or three days, but there was nothing to hold me there.

Within a year I had become a Northerner. I studied to lose my accent and took work as a porter at the New York Central Railroad. Ten years later I had risen to fireman. Twenty years after that I was given a gold-plated watch and twelve dollars a month retirement.

It seemed like a satisfactory amount at the time. And then the Spanish American War set off a round of inflation.

I don't believe the men who set up railway pensions ever expected a body to keep collecting it for thirty years. I've outlived every last one of my colleagues from the railway. And now I've outlived the ability of my pension to support me, but I'm too old to support myself.

I spent the next hour and a half sitting beneath a willow, sacrificing worm after worm to the fishing gods. No business resulted.

I scrabbled around in the damp soil near the crick and came up with some wild onions. Working my way through the underbrush I harvested a handful of left-over summer berries, dried on the bush. I wrapped it all in a hanky and put it in my coat pocket, thinking this was going to make the dangdest-tasting soup I'd ever had.

A sudden cramp doubled me over and I vomited what looked to be coffee grounds. That couldn't be good. I didn't eat coffee grounds. It was clear I needed something in my stomach.

I looked at what I had gathered and decided a mouthful of creek water along with the berries was the right choice.

They weren't sweet, like I'd hoped, maybe a little moldy. I gummed the raisin-like nuggets, swishing them around in my mouth, hoping the water would soften them.

Two minutes later I was puking. Believe me, those berries didn't taste any better coming up than they had going down.

There was nothing for it. I was going to have to importune my niece for a meal. Maybe I could work it off somehow.

V.

> I belong to that highly respectable tribe
> Known as the Shabby Genteel…
> Too proud to beg, too honest to steal.
> *Edward Kidder*

IN 1890, I saw the great comedian Sol Smith Russell performing in the play *A Poor Relation,* down to Cincinnati. At the time I thought it hilarious. Maybe the fact that he had been a drummer boy in the Union Army contributed to my sense of humor. Or maybe just because it was Cincinnati.

Anyway, now that I am myself the poor relation, I realize there wasn't all that much truth to the song. Oh, I'm shabby enough, but I haven't been too honest to steal since the end of the Confederacy. I held out as long as I could on the begging, but I find pride is not nearly so strong as hunger.

I came up to the back of Gladys' place, hoping to speak to her in private. Of course, who should I meet but Darnell, taking out the garbage. I put on my brave face.

"Can I have a word with my niece Gladys?"

"She already gone for the day. Closed up early. She left me here to finish the washing up and latch the doors."

I didn't see how to proceed. I didn't know this man

from Adam's off ox, plus we hadn't got on that well when we first met.

Darnell looked me up and down.

"So I still got the chain gang look? That how you put it?"

"I didn't come here to apologize, but since you brought it up, I have to admit I'm kind of cranky in the mornings."

"I heard you was cranky in the afternoons and evenings, too."

I shrugged. "I've got things to say, but no one cares what an old man thinks. Gets under my skin. I've seen things, I could tell...well, it's just hard."

Darnell reached back into the dark diner and pulled out a pie box.

"Gladys said I was to give this to you, if you should come around."

I am not ashamed to say that a tear leaked out. Darnell saw it, but said nothing.

I opened the box. There was about a third of an apple pie.

"You like apple pie as much as I do?" I said.

"It make a fine dessert."

"I'd offer to share supper with you first, but this pie was going to be my supper."

"That's okay. I already had a samwich from Gladys."

Something was bothering me. As long as I'd known her, Gladys had been a creature of regular habit.

"Why'd she close up early?"

Darnell looked like he wasn't sure how much to tell me.

"See, she hear there might be some trouble in town

tonight. Said the head kluxer tol' her she ought to stay open late, she do some extra business."

This sent a shiver down my spine. Putting it together with what Lars said about the MacKays stirring up a fuss, I preminisced what the night might bring.

"This is probably a night for me to stay off the streets, in fact clear out of town." I said. "Once you get a crowd together in these parts, there are those who find it high-spirited to torment an old man."

Darnell considered that, then spit out his own concern.

"That ain't all. She tol' me I ought to get my *black* ass out of town while it still light."

"As long as I've apologized once, I guess I have to add I'm sorry for that crack about you being a piece of midnight."

"Shee-it, Injun Chief. You just callin' it like you see it."

I looked at the sun, which was about to set. We'd have thirty minutes of dusk, and then night would be upon us.

"Where you headed, Darnell?"

"Down to the settlement. Got me a room there last week when I come up from Virginia."

"If the dumb klucks are running tonight, they may head down there to raise some hell. It's better for your health that they not recognize you from the diner, realize you know their names and faces. Might give them an incentive to keep you silent on a permanent basis."

I could see it in his face: that look of fear, followed by anger, chased by bravado.

"I can take care of myself."

I knew better than to challenge him directly. I'd seen too many of my battle friends go to their deaths with that same attitude.

"Maybe you can help me out a bit. I need to hunt me some meat to go with this pie," I said. "Plus my eyesight at night ain't what it used to be. Let's you and me camp out in the woods, hunt some possum, maybe some raccoon. Stay away from town altogether, keep off the road to the settlement."

"What makes you think I want to camp out with an old geezer like you?"

"Two reasons. I know my way around the woods here and you don't. Also, I'm Uncle Geezer, and you owe it to Gladys."

He looked only about half convinced.

"I just remembered a third reason. I'm going to introduce you to my friend Lars. He's white, lost an arm in the Spanish American War. He fought alongside the Buffalo Regiment in Cuba."

"Buffalo Regiment, huh? Hell, why would I want to be hanging around some one-arm cracker?"

"Cuz he's bringing a bottle of the smoothest corn liquor you ever tasted. As a bonus, he'll tell you a story of how a colored man saved his life at the Battle of El Caney."

"That's a bonus?"

"Well, I doubt you can stop him."

VI.

The woods are made for the hunters of dreams,
The brooks for the fishers of song;
To the hunter who hunts for the gunless game,
The streams and the woods belong.
            The Bloodless Sportsman
                — *Sam Walter Foss*

I SLUNG MY rifle over my shoulder and put four cartridges in my pocket. I tied up two blankets in a roll, put a skinning knife, coffee pot, and a fry pan into a rucksack and I was ready to go.

Darnell had borrowed forks, knives, and three pie tins from the diner. He also had some coffee in a cloth pouch and some salt and pepper twisted into a napkin.

I felt bad about the coffee and the condiments, but figured I'd even things out by drinking one less cup of joe per day for the next week.

Lars had caught up to us while I was packing. As the town drunk, Lars had been the target of enough young toughs to see the wisdom of our campout. He brought the 'shine and draped his blanket about him like a cape. He also wore a top hat I didn't know he owned.

"It suits my style," said Lars. When Darnell gave him a sideways look he added, "Besides, it keeps my head warm."

It was full night and a fog crept up from the creek, leaving droplets on the leaves and twigs. Whenever we brushed foliage we picked up some dew, and soon we were more than a little damp.

"Lars, you realize we're trying to catch some possum or squirrel or raccoon, don't you? We want to have meat for dinner?" I said.

Lars had stopped to wring out the edge of his blanket. He didn't bother answering my question.

"We need to build us a campfire, dry out our stuff," he said. "It's going to get cold tonight and I don't want to sleep wet." He flapped the edge of his blanket as if he thought the movement would help. "Anyhow, I haven't seen any game around here. Why don't we just stop and eat that pie?" He ran his tongue over his lips. "We can chase it with some corn sauce."

"We haven't seed any game," said Darnell, "because you make more damn noise than a diesel tractor."

"We're far enough from town that a fire won't be seen," I said. "Darnell, you and I can go on then and get something for us to cook. But first, let's build it next to that outcropping of schist."

"Outcrop of shits?" said Lars.

"Schist."

"What the hell you talkin' about?" said Darnell.

"When I was a railway fireman I got to know some geology as we traveled through the mountains. It's this stone that comes in layers, has mica in it, you know?"

They didn't and their look told me so. I pointed by way of further explanation.

It took half an hour to get the basic camp set up. Once the fire was going, the stone reflected the heat nicely. Lars began a haphazard job of collecting fuel for the night.

Darnell went over and looked Lars in the eye. "I expect to see every bit of that pie still in the box when we bring back the meat."

"What do you take me for? It's share and share alike," said Lars. "Course, if you don't bring any meat I might have to fill up on sauce."

He began to laugh at his own wit and that turned into a phlegmy cough which probably scared game clear into the next county. Darnell and I left the circle of light while Lars tried to catch his breath.

By the time we had gone two hundred yards, the woods was quiet. I readied my rifle, but truth to tell, I couldn't see well enough to use it. It turned out I didn't need to. Darnell grabbed my arm and put a finger to his lips. He pointed and I saw two possums walking one after the other. They were crossing a fallen log, their tails high, like they had something to be proud of.

Darnell jumped at them and they backed up, mouths gaping, needle-sharp teeth exposed, a hiss like a leaking gas-pipe coming from their ugly mouths. Quicker than I could think about it he grabbed those two possums by their tails, swung 'em around his head and smashed their skulls against the tree trunk.

"Fast work," I said.

"Let's go cook these critters."

"I love roasted possum. Yeah, I s'pose it's the Injun in me."

Darnell gave me a look, until he realized I was funning with him. He showed a mouth full of square, white teeth and we headed on back to Lars.

There are some who think possum is too gamy, and others who think it greasy, and some who think there's too many bones for so little flesh. I'm here to tell you that there isn't much to beat possum roasted over an open fire. We sucked the grease from our fingers, and I saw Darnell skin the meat from the tail bone with his teeth. We didn't leave much but fur and fangs behind.

With possum, coffee, and apple pie inside, we all felt considerable better. We put our backs against the outcrop, soaking up the heat of the fire, smoking hand-rolled cigarettes. Lars broke out the bottle of Granny's middling quality rye and we passed it around, telling yarns. To our mutual satisfaction we discovered that all three of us were veterans. That set off another round of tall tales.

After some time I noticed that Darnell had gone quiet.

"Is that possum not sitting right?" I said. "You feeling sick, nephew?"

Lars sat up at that. I hadn't told him that Darnell and I were related.

"My people once were warriors in Africa, brave. They kill lions. Use the two-edged ida, fight with the curved agedengbe." He took a pull from the bottle. "Me, I'm in 809th Pioneer Infantry. In the white man's army they din't give me no weapons. I had no sword. I shame my name, Ogbe Baba. Two years I unload ships in France, like a slave. After the war, there wasn't no parade for Negro soldiers."

"S'not true." Lars belched and waved his hand. "I saw a Negro troop get a welcome in Harlem that turned into a three day party."

"Not in Virginia. White man afraid we gon' take his job now we back from war, got some skills. They make sure we don' get no work."

Lars showed little sympathy. "No one made you go back to ole Virginny."

Darnell's look darkened even more. "I saw a northern nigger, didn't know no better. He wanted to eat in the train station. They try to throw him out and he say he a veteran. He say he shed his blood for this country, so he gon' eat where he want. They lynch him an' he still got his uniform on."

"You're telling me they lynched a veteran, and he was still wearing his uniform?" said Lars, shaking his head.

"I seen it myself," said Darnell. "I ain't ashame to say I cried."

"It ain't right," I said. "Them whites claim we're all created equal, but look at the way they treat the coloreds and the Indians."

Darnell threw a pinecone into the night. Something skittered away into the brush.

"Why we hiding in the forest like animals?" said Darnell. "I'm a man."

"Of course you are a man. We are all men here," I tried to put a good face on it. "Smart men who will live to be older."

"It is not right to hide in the forest," said Darnell.

I recognized his feelings but knew better than to commiserate. There was no solace for his pain, the loss of his birthright.

In fact, the more I thought about it, the worse I felt about my own birthright.

I was the descendant of Cherokee warriors and here I was afraid to show my face in town. It was intolerable. I sought refuge in memory.

"I was raised with the ten commandments, thou shalt not kill and all," I said. "But when I joined the army they told me it was all right with God if I killed those sons of bitches on the other side. I guess I believed my commanding officers, more so than the Bible."

Darnell stared at me. "What war was that?"

"War Between the States. I killed until I could kill no more. There were days on end when I couldn't rid my nostrils of the smell of blood and gunpowder and shit." I put my hand out for the bottle. "I'll never forget the first time I fired my rifle in anger. I had no glimmer of what it would mean to pull the trigger and watch that boy in blue fall down."

"Boy in blue?" said Darnell. "What side you on?"

I ignored him. "I told myself that lots of men were firing, I couldn't be sure it was my round that had snuffed out his life."

"Part injun, part Nigra and you a johnny reb?" There was disbelief in Darnell's voice.

"When it got dark I crawled out and found his body. He wasn't no more than sixteen, maybe a year older than me. Looked like a nice fellow, like we could have been friends in other circumstances."

"Cain't believe what I heared," said Darnell. "You related to me, you part Negro, and you one a them."

"You don't know a damn thing, Darnell. There were thousands of Negro troops wearing the gray."

"Bull."

"Maybe you'd know better if you'd been there," I said, feeling defensive. "I was fighting to keep North Carolina free, protect my mama's home."

"Ain't no excuse."

I waited, stubbing out the remains of my cigarette. I thought about it at length. I took a ragged breath.

"Yeah, you're right."

I lapsed into silence.

"At least you both came back with all your limbs," said Lars. "You try getting work when you have one arm, veteran or no."

Darnell and I waited for Lars to go on. It took him about three medium-size swallows before he was ready.

"My parents came from Norway in 1880. I was raised on tales of Vikings, the fiercest warriors ever to have fought."

Darnell and I both protested at this. Lars waved his hands and shushed us.

"I know, I know. Everybody thinks their own ancestors were the mightiest warriors. But the Vikings did have something special, the berserkers."

"The what?"

"It means bear shirts, comes from the days when the Norse wore bear skins into battle, a wolf head for a helmet. They'd go crazy in battle, fearless, attack anything, couldn't feel pain, couldn't be stopped."

"Sound like my cousin when he drunk," said Darnell.

"It wasn't like that at all," said Lars. "We'd been in a trench all day in the sun, and the damned Spaniards had been shooting down on us from the flank of San Juan Hill. I thought my brains were going to fry. I drank my canteen dry. We fought our way uphill, taking casualties at every step. I was so hot I felt faint.

"I stripped off my jacket. I unbuttoned my shirt. I couldn't see where to aim, what with the sweat running down into my eyes, and the Spanish had smokeless powder for their Mausers. I got angrier and angrier and then they called out to charge over the Spanish embankment and I went wild. I shot until I ran out of ammunition, so I resorted to my bayonet.

"The Spanish were low on ammo, too, and they were fighting with bayonets and knives. One of them hit me in the head with his rifle butt. My cap was knocked off, but it served to deflect the force of the blow. Still, it opened my scalp and the blood ran down my face and into my eyes and I couldn't see. I must have been a sight though. I began to scream and jab with my rifle."

His breath came in little gasps now. Darnell and I were still as mice.

"My bayonet stuck in some fellow's breastbone. I tried to jerk it out, but it wouldn't turn loose. I yanked his rifle out of his hands by the barrel and used it like a club to smash the heads of the men in the trench. A man pulled his pistol and put it against my arm and fired and I never even felt my arm fly away.

"I saw the blood spurting from my stump and jumped the man with the pistol and pushed my knife through his eye into his brain. I could see his mouth open and his tongue working, but I couldn't hear a sound. I could see nothing except the next man to kill."

Sweat poured down his face. Maybe tears, too.

"It went on and on until I lost so much blood I blacked out." He glanced at his empty sleeve. "They gave me a medal and an honorable discharge and a disability pension. Just enough to keep me in drink or groceries, but not both."

He raised the bottle to his lips and downed the last ounce of 120 proof rye.

"Guess we know how that turned out."

The tears streamed down his face now. He turned away from us and put his head down.

There was nothing to say, so we kept still.

Within seconds Lars was snoring like a freight train. He had escaped once again.

VII.

In this circle
Oh ye warriors
Lo, I tell you
Each his future.
> *Song of the Seer*
> — *Tatanka-Ptecila*

TWENTY MINUTES WALKING got us completely out of sight and sound of Lars. We were planning on getting some game for the morning pot.

Darnell moved well in the darkness, and I could see he had done some hunting before. The fog began to thin and the moon came out, so we had better visibility.

We were headed towards a hollow I knew about. It usually had plenty of tracks in it because of the moist ground. The gap in the tree canopy there meant plenty of bushes for animals to eat. We made our way in companionable silence, him following my lead.

Darnell smelled it before I did.

"Something burning," he said.

I sniffed. There it was, faint but certain.

"Isn't that from our campfire?"

"Naw. It not wood smoke. That kerosene."

We walked on for some minutes trying to figure what was up. Again, Darnell was first to note something.

"Hear that?"

I stopped stock still, held my breath. I could make out some commotion, but it was still too faint for me to discover what it might be.

"What is it?"

"Sound like people. A lot of 'em."

And then came the scream. That high yowl pierced the night like an arrow. We waited, hardly breathing. The scream went on and on.

"We ought to get back to Lars," I said. "Put that fire out and hunker down for the night."

"I think we need see what that all about."

"One of the reasons I got to be an old man is because I learned to walk the opposite direction when I hear bad things."

"I ain't old man yet." Darnell squared his shoulders. "I'm going. You do what you—"

At that moment there was a noise in the brush twenty yards behind me. Darnell looked over my shoulder and his face went tight.

A dog burst out of the sumac, running full tilt like the devil was after him. There was a rope of saliva hanging from his muzzle, and as he flew by I saw a patch of hair matted with blood at the base of his skull. He was making a sound I never heard from a dog before, a low growl that was almost a moan. The dog raced by, not even glancing at us.

"What?" said Darnell. I could see the whites of his eyes. "What that?"

"I believe that was Marshal Lawe's dog, Chief."

"You see that blood? That drool hanging from his mouth?" said Darnell. "That a Hell hound."

I hitched my britches and set off after Chief. Darnell

fell in next to me. We started at a trot, but as we got closer to the noise of the crowd we slowed down, circled a bit, and came out on a slight rise overlooking the hollow. There was a sudden hullabaloo accompanied by frenzied barking.

I stared toward the bonfire, but with my eyesight I couldn't really make out what was going on.

Darnell could, though. He stared for a long minute, his mouth working. Then he turned to the side and vomited into the bushes.

About then the screaming stopped.

"What did you see, Darnell?" I whispered. "My eyes, you know."

"They done lynched a man down there and then burn him alive. His body still hanging. And they's folks fighting, too."

I didn't know what to say to that. I'd seen lynchings before, but I didn't think Darnell would want to hear my tales. And I didn't care to explain further to him why I'd fought under the Stars and Bars.

We stayed hidden up on the rise and watched as the crowd dispersed and the fire died down.

An hour later there was just one man left. Well, I guess two, if you count the dead one.

Darnell and I moved closer, silent as death, right up to the edge of the firelight. I wanted to see if I recognized who had been killed. I don't know why Darnell stayed with me.

Darnell was weeping as we walked, though he made not a sound.

A crow flickered by overhead. It moved from branch to branch, seeming to parallel our approach to the clearing.

I whispered to Darnell. "You ever see a crow moving about at night like that?"

He looked at me, his cheeks wet with tears, his mouth a rictus of pain.

"That not a crow. That a fetch, come to take this man's soul straight to Hell."

The crow—for that's what I still believed it to be—soared down from atop a maple and lighted on the head of the still smoking corpse. The bird craned his neck until it looked straight into the face of the dead man. It plucked out the eyes one by one, swallowing with what seemed to be pure avian joy. I began to think Darnell might be on to something.

And then the crow let out one tremendous kaw, a kaw of triumph, like it thought it was monarch of the forest.

The living man in the clearing had been dozing, but the sound awoke him and he turned to see where this unholy cry had come from. When he did, both Darnell and I recognized Jedediah Spout.

I backed into the darkness, not wanting to be seen by the man I knew to be the Kleagle.

"Let's get away from here, Darnell," I said, pitching my voice low.

Darnell's eyes were stony.

"You go. But leave the rifle with me."

GRANNY MACKAY

As the twig is bent the tree inclines.
— *Virgil*

I.

CALL ME MEHITABEL.

That seemed to work for Melville, but I find it awkward, especially now that all those who might have addressed me thus are gone. My parents and siblings are dead, the girlfriends of my childhood have either passed away or moved to other places. I buried my beloved husband five years ago.

He called me Hetty.

So don't call me Mehitabel, after all. No one else does.

Call me Granny, like they all do.

There are some folk who say that I am a kind and caring woman. Such folk would be wrong. I am a business woman, the most successful in the state of Massachusetts. I run the largest moonshine operation in the three western counties.

And I do not give credit. My operations are strictly cash.

However, I can be warm and generous. If you are my kin.

Even then, do not cross me.

IT WAS ONLY three days ago this all began. I remember I had to push my daughter aside to get a clearer view of my grandson's bloody back.

"Stop blubbering, Letty Jo. Get me those needle-nose

pliers and the ice pick from the drawer by the dry sink. I need to get this birdshot out."

Letty Jo dabbed at her eyes with the cuff of her sleeve and sniffled into her hanky. She went to get the tools while I used what remained of Andrew's shirt to wipe away the blood and get a better view of the damage. Andrew winced away from my touch, but made no sound.

Jackson, Letty Jo's near-mute other half, barreled through the front door and dropped onto the divan, sweat running from his scalp and mingling with blood seeping from half a dozen perforations in his face and neck. He was white as a sheet and said nothing, just uncorked a jug of our special brew, and drank deep. When he came up for air he muttered something about "that dago," then lapsed into silence.

Moments later, two of my nephews came in from the drive lugging Angus between them. Angus was unconscious, bleeding heavily. I hurried over, pulled off his shirt and saw that he had been peppered with more than fifty pellets. I knew it was more than I could handle here.

"You boys get him down to the county hospital. I cannot patch up all three of them by myself, and he looks like he took the worst of it."

"Yes, ma'am," said my sister's boy. "Course, this means that the law might get involved."

I looked at him in wonder. "We have three men with gunshot wounds—"

"No, six," he said. "Already dropped three by my folks' place."

"When six people have been shot, I think you can pretty much count on the law taking an interest. Who else was hurt?"

Two more grandsons and another nephew. At the time it appeared as if we were involved in a trade war with our rival distiller, Nick DeCosta.

It turned out to be much more stupid than that.

"Get Angus into the car and have your brother drive him. I want you to stay behind and explain."

Letty Jo handed me the pliers and an ice pick, then put a mug of 200 proof next to me. I swished the tools in the alcohol then wiped them clean on a new-washed square of cloth cut from the curtains I had just replaced.

I took the pick and probed the first puncture on Andrew's back. A wave of muscle contraction shimmied down the flesh of his back and I heard Letty Jo gulp for air, then puke onto my new rag rug.

"Oh for land's sake! If you cannot be of any help just get away!" I said. "No, wait. First get a towel and a bucket and clean up your mess. I do not want this rug smelling to high heaven just because you have a delicate stomach."

"I'm sorry, Ma."

"I do not see how you managed to give birth to six children, yet still cannot stand the sight of blood."

She slunk off and I put the pick back into Andrew, feeling around to find the pellet. Once I tapped it, I switched to the needle-nose pliers, and pulled it out. Andrew tried not to squirm and never let out a peep.

I was proud of his stoicism, but wished he had more brains than brawn. He and his twin brother Angus were named after my late husband, Angus Andrew MacKay. They thought that fisticuffs could solve most arguments, despite a plethora of previous wounds. They seemed incapable of learning from experience.

IT TOOK AWHILE for my nephew to get the story out, and Letty Jo's husband was useless for adding any detail. Seems that my eighteen-year-old grandsons had been at a church social, selling some of our sour mash special to the local Baptists.

That only made good business sense. Since Prohibition we have had more trade than ever. I understand that before the Volstead Act there were something like one thousand saloons and bars in this state. Now that the act is federal law our fair state has six thousand speakeasies.

As a side benefit, I no longer have to worry about avoiding excise tax. Since moonshine is illegal, it cannot be sold. If it cannot be sold, it cannot be taxed.

Though my father was Presbyterian, some of my sisters had married Baptists, Methodists, Episcopalians, and whatnot. As long as they weren't Papists, Anglicans, or Jews they were all right with Father. Which is just a long way of saying that whichever church was having a social, some of my kin were attending as members.

And that means that some of my sons, grandsons, or nephews can wangle an invitation and make sales from the trunk of a Model T automobile. The Baptist pastors were always the ones who got most pissy about this, but too many of their congregants had developed a taste for MacKay goods for them to be able to put a halt to it.

I noticed that mostly it was the womenfolk who objected to their men drinking our moonshine. I put this down to a remark concerning drink which the porter made in *Macbeth*—that while it provoked desire, it took away performance.

Be that as it may, Angus and Andrew were at the social when they spied their cousin Jackie Sue Palmer going off into the bushes with some young blood they did not recognize. Jackie Sue is only thirteen, but like her mother she had ripened early and could easily pass for eighteen.

Angus and Andrew, being only eighteen themselves, had been casting their eyes upon her for the last year, trying to figure out if having the same great-grandpa made her too close a relation to court. They had come to me pretending to be interested in family history, trying to ascertain if she were marriageable.

I had attempted to explain to them that the church— and the law in most states—frowned upon marriages between cousins. They were more confused after my explanation of consanguinity than they were before I started.

That was the moment I realized they were destined to be the next generation of muscle in the MacKay operation, not the new management.

In any case, Angus had followed Jackie Sue into the bushes where he caught the young man with his hands well inside her bodice, while Jackie Sue had her fingers busy inside the boy's pants. He grabbed the young man by the ear and dragged him out of the shrubbery, doing his best to twist the auricle clean off the boy's head. The boy fought back, drawing a crowd.

Meanwhile Jackie Sue ran screaming to her parents that she had been interfered with. A mob soon formed, and the lad got a good beating.

I lost track of the narrative here, but one fact became clear: the troublesome boy from the next county was a grandson of mine, a boy I had never met by the name of Angus DeCosta. He was the offspring of my youngest daughter, Mary Elizabeth.

I saw this matter wouldn't be put to rest easily, and so I began to think about what to do next. The MacKays needed a plan.

II.

Young men, hear an old man
to whom old men hearkened
when he was young.
— *Caesar Augustus*

MY FAMILY HAD been losing custom to Nick DeCosta
for the last decade, and I wanted to put a stop to it. Oh,
our farm is profitable enough, feeds the family well, with
rich land that yields tall maize and rich grass for the dairy
kine. But our real source of cash comes from the corn
byproduct for which we are justly famous. My husband
brought a skill to brewing poteen that bordered on the
miraculous.

We once calculated, with the help of a family Bible
that had come over on a sailing ship, that my Angus
was probably the tenth generation distiller of corn mash
in his family. It was in his blood. And to hear him or his
father talk of that "Barstard" King Charles, you would
have thought that particular monarch was still alive and
collecting excise.

My own father never allowed his children to read any
books save the King James Bible or Shakespeare, though
I became an avid reader of the classics after I married.
By some obscure reasoning this also meant that we were
not allowed to use contractions in our speech.

My father had many rules for his children. I have not yet been able to shake off his stricture against contractions.

Nor had my father thought it becoming for girls to attend school beyond the sixth reader. So I had never heard of this King Charles.

My son's eighth grade history teacher enlightened me. King Charles of England—and Ireland too, or so he presumed—had imposed his hated tax on distilled liquors in 1642. Two hundred and seventy years later the MacKays still cursed his name. And they thought the U.S. Internal Revenue Service was nothing more than the same interference with private income here in the New World.

I have heard that Henry Ford says history is bunk, but I guess this proves otherwise. The Scotch-Irish, at least, have very long memories and I suppose that counts as history.

On the other hand, Mr. Ford appears to have more money than God, while my son's history teacher can't even afford to buy one of the automobiles that Mr. Ford produces. All he owns can be put in the pockets of his single threadbare suit.

But which one of the two is happier? The multimillionaire who disbelieves in history or the impecunious teacher who does? Five years ago I put the question to my Angus as he lay upon his death bed. We both had a good chuckle, and I think it may have been my husband's last bit of pleasure before he passed.

III.

It was a wine jar when the molding began:
as the wheel runs round,why does it turn out
as a water pitcher?
Ars Poetica
— *Horace*

THE NEXT DAY I took Angus and Andrew into town to meet with Judge Halbertson. I believed that we could prevent an unpleasant courtroom spectacle if we got the principals together and threshed things out.

"I'm afraid the situation has gone beyond that point, Mrs. MacKay. The county prosecutors in both Jefferson and Potemkin have already filed cases," said the judge. "These young men will have to stand trial."

Angus and Andrew looked as forlorn as puppies caught with their noses in the pot roast.

"But they have had other brushes with the law," I said. "Can we not pay a fine and expunge this youthful indiscretion from their records?"

Angus and Andrew perked up.

"That was possible in previous instances," said the judge. "But now that they are eighteen, they have been charged as adults. And charged with attempted murder, mind you. This is a serious case."

The boys cast their eyes down in despair.

"What about the fact that Nicolas DeCosta attempted to murder them? Or does a shotgun not count as a serious attempt?"

Angus and Andrew looked up, full of hope.

"Of course it does. That's why they'll be testifying in Mr. DeCosta's trial in Jefferson County. But that doesn't change things here in Potemkin. They'll stand trial in two days."

I saw panic in the boys' eyes. I realized they could not control their emotions and their every thought was written bold on their faces. My god, but they were only a short step from being simples.

ONE OF THE side effects of age is the flood of memory that accompanies every event, each one calling to mind similar episodes from the past. I remember my grandmother saying that it felt as if she stood at the edge of a waterfall. New events swept by too quickly to contemplate, while past times swirled about familiarly.

Be that as it may, I have been thinking about my childhood and the stories I was told. Mother was Irish Catholic and married a Protestant Scot in Ulster, possibly losing her soul in the process. I was never clear whether she thought herself damned or not, but she certainly lost all contact with her family. They shunned her and acted as if she had died—no, rather that she had never been born.

The day she threw in her lot with Melchizedek MacAllister was the last she ever saw of her mother and father and kin. A month later, she being already pregnant, they were aboard ship on the way to America.

She told me and my siblings this story so often that I have never been a stranger to the idea of familial loss.

Father was Presbyterian and a strict Calvinist, as you might have guessed from his name. He was clear in his mind as to who was saved and who was damned to eternal hellfire. The latter group greatly outnumbered the former.

It galled Father greatly that he had fallen in love with a near-pagan Catholic, but he found her to be biddable and fecund. That seemed to be enough for him.

Of course, I learned much of this secondhand from my aunts and uncles. Father never deigned to spend much time speaking to me or my sisters. Our job was to do the truck farming, keep the house clean, sit up straight in church, tend to the needs of our brothers, and help Mother with the littler ones.

Each of my sisters married as soon as possible to establish her own household and get out from under the cloud of anger and depression that clung to my father. Father always demanded to meet each daughter's prospective beau. He would tell the young man that he would watch him carefully, but I think he was just relieved there would soon be one less mouth to feed.

I HATED MY name, Mehitabel, and was known as Hetty to my friends. Once, when I was thirteen, I mentioned this at dinner. My father reached across and slapped me, telling me that I dare not foreshorten a name from the Holy Bible. Mother winced, but she didn't speak up. Like myself, she knew better than to cry or show any emotion; Melchizadek never did. I kept my own counsel from then on.

I promised myself that very night that I would begin looking seriously at the boys in our county, to see which of them might be ready to marry in two years.

Angus MacKay had seemed the most likely prospect. Big boned, not too handsome, a third son, awkward and shy—the prettier girls would not be chasing him.

AND SO, TWENTY-SIX months later, Angus and his father made a formal visit to our farm and asked to speak to Father. Mother got them all glasses of sarsaparilla, which I served, then took me outdoors to execute some minor chores with the chickens. The men settled their business between themselves, then came outside.

Angus was red as a beet and would not look me in the eye, nor would my mother. I feared things had gone awry, but the two fathers shook hands heartily, as though they had concluded a business deal that was satisfactory to each. The two MacKays got into their buggy—a nice dogcart, pulled by a sturdy-looking gelding—and left.

Angus was invited to attend the Presbyterian church with us and share a meal with the family on the following Sunday. When he arrived in a new suit, his hair freshly cut, and wearing a four-in-hand tie, I thought he looked almost handsome.

After the service my father took him aside for a walk in the church cemetery, during which Angus looked nervous and serious at the same time. Mother and I waited in the buckboard, saying nothing, because what did we have to say, after all.

My younger siblings prattled behind us, unmindful that my fate was being determined a few yards away.

I swore that I would never grow to be like my mother. When I had children, I would defend my young against all harm.

Thirty minutes later the two men took their places on the front seat, my father flicking the reins, and we proceeded home.

After that Sunday Father took no more interest in Angus McKay, my husband-to-be, than he had any of the other suitors to my sisters. Mother, though, took me aside for a little talk.

"Mehitabel, I wonder if you have truly discerned this young man's character." She paused for effect.

I was puzzled but said nothing. She would get around to whatever was bothering her in her own good time.

"I don't mean to criticize your father, but men do not see everything that a woman sees." She seemed to search for words. "Or smells."

She had my attention. "Smells?"

"I smelled alcohol on Mr. MacKay when he came to speak to your father. And other times on young Angus."

"I don't believe Angus drinks, Mother."

"Possibly not. It wasn't on his breath, but the odor was on his clothes and in his hair."

"I would prefer it if you did not sniff my beau, Mother. It is very forward and lacks gentility."

She colored, and I saw that I had angered her. "It was as I leaned over him to serve the butter beans that I recognized it," she said.

"Whatever are you speaking of?" I realized that my voice was sharp.

My mother was startled that I had shown such

effrontery. Her face stiffened and she pulled away from me.

"I see that being affianced has made you willful. I suppose you will have to learn some truths on your own."

She turned away and left me alone, wondering if I now would have to ask my sisters regarding the secrets of the wedding night.

Some days later my sister Clarabelle dropped by with her new bairn, a puling mound of flesh that was all eyes, ears, and foul emanations. I took her aside while Mother made a huge fuss over the baby.

What I heard more or less confirmed what I already suspected from events I had witnessed around the barnyard, but none of it involved the odor of alcohol. My sister went so far as to ask if I was daft when I brought that particular subject up.

And so I found out Angus MacKay and his father had a distillery two days after I was no longer a virgin. Neither was a thrill at the time, but I accommodated both.

I even came to enjoy these indulgences.

IV.

A pauper in the midst of wealth.
— *Horace*

OVER THE NEXT forty years my husband and I had prospered. When the weather was good, our farm flourished. When times were hard for other farmers, the MacKays always had the still to provide income. We owned one of the few farms in the county without a mortgage.

I gave birth to ten children and seven of them grew to have their own families. Some became farmers, or farmer's wives, some went to work in factories in other cities.

And of course there was my youngest, Mary Elizabeth. She had been the apple of her father's eye. I warned him over and over that he was spoiling her, but he was besotted with the child. I have to admit she was the prettiest of my babies and smart as a whip. It was our greatest sorrow when she became so wild and ran off with that Italian.

And then the grandchildren! They helped to assuage the loss of our daughter, though not a day went by that I did not think of her.

I suppose our story is common enough. But it was our own tragedy and so it was more real to us than those others we only heard of through gossip.

Ten years ago Angus fell to the ground unconscious one day as he was working. When he awoke, the right side of his face no longer moved in a proper fashion and he had great difficulty speaking. Seldom could he put an entire sentence together without help from those around him.

The stroke changed his personality. He spent much more time playing with his grandchildren and tussling with the dogs. He lost all interest in farm work and I had to hire help.

He never lost his touch at mixing mash, though. However, I foresaw that another stroke would relieve him of even the remnants of personality he yet had. I watched him prepare a batch for the still and wrote down detailed instructions, that I might not lose his recipes.

He seemed to find it amusing that I helped him with the still, but he was also grateful for the assistance. He could no longer lift the grain and sugar bags as before.

When he passed five years ago I felt a great stone move into my chest and settle there.

With the children grown and without the moderating influence of my late husband I discovered my talent for business. I have a special gift for driving bargains and spotting opportunities, particularly among those colleagues who have fallen on hard times.

For those who think to cheat me, they find that I have more large Celtic menfolk among my kin than they can shake a stick at. It is much more likely that my kin will shake a stick at them.

By the way, that is what my family calls "Granny's sense of humor."

BIG BILL SYKES

Avarice, ambition, lust, etc.,
are nothing but species of madness.
Theological-Political Treatise
— Spinoza

I.

"BOTH OF US know they were trying to kill the DeCosta boy, Herman," I said. "You'd be better served if you got them to plead guilty."

Herman Schneider might have been a public defender but he wasn't a fool. I add that the only job he could secure was public defender, not county prosecutor.

We were sitting in Judge Halbertson's chambers waiting for the old man to come out of the toilet and finish his pre-trial instructions. My case was strong against the MacKay brothers, but Herman wasn't about to play dead.

"Plead guilty to attempted murder?" said Herman. "That would send them to the state penitentiary for seven years. If I let them plead to that the MacKays'll nail my hide to the courthouse door." He looked up at me with sly eyes. "Besides, you're going to have to convince the jury that there was premeditated intent to kill the DeCosta boy. And most of that jury is kin to the defendants."

"Kinship isn't the key here," I said. "You think I can't sway that jury? I took my degree in psychology before I entered law school. The psychology of juries is just a special case of the psychology of mobs. I'll have these rubes howling for blood by the time I'm done with summation."

Herman's grin changed from sly to frozen as he contemplated that. He looked at his shoes as if he thought there might be a solution stuck to the bottom.

But in my heart I feared that Herman was right and the MacKay boys' kin were going to let them off. I thought it worth my time to see if I couldn't intimidate him before we went to trial. I'd prosecuted enough cases in this county to know that once we got into the courtroom a lot of things could go the wrong way.

"What was your pre-law major, Herman? Didn't I hear it was architecture?"

He set his mouth firmly, not rising to the bait.

"Seems your folks wouldn't pay for you to attend college unless you studied for the bar?" I continued, reminding him yet again that this wasn't his choice of profession, but Mommy and Daddy's.

"It wasn't that they didn't have the money to send you. They did, but there were strings attached, weren't there?" I set the barb. "I didn't have your advantages. I had to work my way through State on my own. Fortunately I won enough scholarships to make it possible."

Herman gave me a nasty simper. "That's the great thing about our state colleges. They may not be first rank schools, but they do their best to help the disadvantaged take a step up from their origins. I believe I heard they are going to start awarding scholarships to our Negro citizens of academic talent."

I hadn't heard this and it made me seethe with rage. It was another political action that would discredit the value of my degree. No doubt the ploy was being used to garner the colored vote in the big cities.

The sooner I could put this penny ante town and its precious little job behind me, the better. I had bigger ambitions.

"What if I reduced the charge to aggravated assault?"

I said. "The boys wouldn't do more than twelve to eighteen months."

"You can get Judge Halbertson to guarantee that sentence?"

And there he had me. Halbertson was unpredictable. His sentences depended on his mood, and his mood depended upon how much he'd had to drink the night before. These days that was usually plenty. When I got to the legislature my first order of business would be removing these old sots from the bench.

Herman saw my indecision, though I tried to mask it. He gloated to himself and took off his glasses to polish them on his silk tie.

I needed a new angle.

The judge came out of the tiny private bathroom that opened off his chambers, wiping his hands on a paper towel and looking pleased with himself. You'd have thought he'd just solved a quadratic equation or translated a passage from Herodotus.

He looked at Herman and said, "Did you get that letter from the Yale Alumni Association?"

"I didn't open mine yet, Judge."

"There's going to be a Thanksgiving celebration this year, get all our most successful classmates together again. Makes me think there's going to be another fundraiser. Still, it would be good to see the old boys again."

Halbertson looked my way and seemed to remember that we were all there to try a case. He motioned us to chairs and took out a folder.

We spent a joyless half hour listening to his almost coherent rambling about rules and procedures. It gave me time to think about how to advance my political career.

II.

I do not speak to the weak:
they want to obey and
lapse into slavery quickly.
— *Friedrich Nietzsche*

AMERICA'S A BIG country, but it's full of little towns populated by small minds. Far too few of our citizens see the big picture. It's just as well that only a fraction of them exercise their franchise in any particular election.

It is fatuous to pretend that the citizenry governs the country in any substantive way.

Although it contradicts the very foundations of democracy, it is the wealthy and elite who govern this broad land. However, they do it well, and it is well that they do.

My parents were hardscrabble farmers in western Massachusetts, and I attended public school. Though I was a member of the honor society, and editor of the school newspaper, that public school diploma and state college degree continue to mark me as an outsider among those who wield power in this state.

I'm going to change that.

I've been county prosecutor for five years. At thirty

years old I've been eligible to serve in the state senate for the last five years.

And now I believe I have the issue that will get me into the senate. Who knows, with a break or two, I could go from there to the governor's office.

It was 1924 when the Klan held that big rally in Worcester, not so far from here. Twenty-four thousand of those dumb klucks paraded around by torchlight. They even hired a red biplane to fly overhead, but some sharpshooter brought that down with a few well-placed shots.

Eight hundred Knights of the KKK came down by truck from the Maine Klavern to make sure no outsiders tried to break up the konvocation. For a while it looked like they might make good on their promise to sweep the Irish Catholics out of office, at least in the western half of the state. They figured if they got things going in the farm counties it could grow into a recall movement to clean out the corrupt government in Boston, perhaps even clear out the Capitol.

It wasn't to be. I know where this state is headed. It's been clear to me ever since the Kennedys got started. That's the wagon I'm getting on.

Anyway, on that particular night in Worcester someone turned the Knights of Columbus loose. After all the broken heads and burned cars, the Klan declined in popularity.

But they're not gone. They're just licking their wounds and biding their time. That rally in Indianapolis of four hundred thousand Klansmen, the march in full regalia in front of the Washington monument serve to show the numbers that are still out there.

They are a potent symbol.

If they were to make a comeback, it would be a backward development for this country. So if a certain prosecutor were instrumental in stopping them...

I can see an anti-bigotry candidate going far. All I need is for this case to turn ugly and provide the springboard.

III.

If you wish to drown, do not torture yourself
with shallow water.
— *Bulgarian proverb*

ANGUS DECOSTA WAS the first witness in the trial.
He wore a cast on his left leg and elastic bandages on
his right. He came up the aisle of the courtroom in a
wheelchair, then used a crutch to get situated in the
witness chair. He sported a largish bruise on the side
of his neck. He was a good-looking lad and the gallery
seemed sympathetic to him as he was sworn in.

"State your name and place of residence for the record,"
said Herman Schneider.

"Angus Nicola DeCosta. I live at 425 Sycamore in Mills
Gap."

Herman leaned in close to the boy, like he was a
friend.

"I understand you are related to the MacKays of
Potemkin County."

"Yes, sir. MacKay is my mother's maiden name."

"And your parents are?"

"Mary Elizabeth MacKay DeCosta and Nicola Antony
David DeCosta." He pronounced it Dah-veed.

"Had you ever met any of the MacKays before the
day in question?"

"My daddy was of the opinion it was better not to waste our time on the MacKays, them being such pri— uhhh, them being so prejudiced."

"Your father thinks the MacKays are prejudiced?"

I got to my feet. "Objection, your honor. Hearsay."

"Sustained."

DeCosta looked around expectantly after I had interrupted, as if he expected the bailiff to take his billy club to the defense lawyer. When nothing further happened, he said. "Yeah, 'cause the MacKays hate Catholics, and Italians, and Jews."

Someone in the back of the courtroom called out, "Well, who don't?" A spasm of laughter rippled through the courtroom.

The judge gaveled the room to silence.

"Another outburst like that and I will charge whoever does so with contempt of court."

The bailiff stood and glared into every corner of the courtroom as if the force of his gaze would make the culprit fess up.

"Young man," said Judge Halbertson, "when I sustain an objection from counsel, you are not to answer the question."

"What question?"

I hid my amusement. Herman must have wanted to get this kid off the stand as soon as possible, but he needed a particular bit of testimony in the record. He was going to have to put up with the kid's nonsense.

"Mr. DeCosta, had you ever met Jackie Sue Palmer before?"

Angus didn't answer, just looked expectantly at me.

We all waited for a few moments. Finally the Judge cleared his throat.

"Please answer the question, Mr. DeCosta."

"I was waiting for the other guy to object again. I thought maybe I wasn't supposed to answer."

"Answer unless instructed otherwise."

"Okay then. I had never met Jackie Sue Palmer before."

"So you were unaware that she was a relative of yours?" said Herman.

"Why would I care about that?"

"I didn't say you should care. I asked if you knew she was a relative."

"I did not know," he said, simpering. "Or care."

This young man exuded bad boy charisma. I looked at the gallery and noticed the Rameson's twin thirteen-year-old girls making eyes at DeCosta. I saw him wink back at them. I'm glad to say they had the grace to blush. Their mother pulled a hairbrush out of her pocketbook, reached across, and smacked the girls on the backs of their hands.

"So you made an appearance at a church social to which you were not invited?"

"Yessir." He was getting cute now.

"And you partook of the food that was laid out there, though you had brought nothing to share?"

"Do I look like a cook to you?" said Angus.

"Answer the question that is asked, young man," said Halbertson.

"I brought nothing to share because I didn't know I would be attending a church social. I came across into Potemkin County on a dare."

"A dare?"

"Cletus Roarke said he didn't think I had the stones to show my face across the county line, on account of he'd heard how my parents had scooted out of there back before I was born."

Halbertson was befuddled a moment, then rapped his gavel.

"You'll keep a civil tongue, young man. There are women and children present."

"I'm just answering the question that was asked, your highness."

Angus smirked again and Halbertson flushed a nice shade of mauve. I could see the thirst rising within him. Herman hurried on.

"How did you make Miss Palmer's acquaintance?"

"Wasn't hard."

Herman ground his teeth. "Let us not cast aspersions on the young lady. Tell me how you met her."

"I've been told I have a certain amount of charm," said Angus. He gave a lazy, and thoroughly obnoxious, smile. "Ladies seem to come to meet me. I don't have to chase after them."

I scanned the room and saw that all the mothers in the audience had pursed their lips and tightened their grip on their handbags. Doctor Freud would have been pleased to see his theories thus confirmed. Three of them rose to their feet and dragged their respective daughters out of the courtroom.

The fathers in the audience were stony-faced. Only the single men looked at Angus with bemused, or perhaps envious, expressions.

"All right, you met in some fashion. And then some time later you were under the rhododendron bush with her. How did that come about?"

"It was uncomfortable in the sun, plus the little kids were buzzing around us like flies. I told Jackie Sue we could have some privacy if we ducked into the bushes."

Herman just about licked his chops. "You told her you wanted to have some privacy with her." He cast a look at the jury, indicating what he thought of DeCosta's depraved morality. "Were you aware that Miss Palmer is only thirteen? Thirteen!" he said, an Old Testament prophet-like thunder in his voice.

"You telling me that girl is just thirteen? And she's already got bosoms like that? Must be something in the water over here in Potemkin, because the melons sure ripen early."

It took three minutes for the uproar to die down after that statement. Halbertson gaveled his arm sore and called a fifteen minute recess so he could find some rubbing alcohol. Whether he chafed with it or drank it is still an open question.

IV.

Virtue is harder to be got than knowledge
of the world; and if lost in a young man,
is seldom recovered.
Some Thoughts Concerning Education
— *John Locke*

WHEN WE RECONVENED Herman continued questioning DeCosta.

"I'm going to ask something personal now. I want you to answer only what I ask. Judge Halbertson has already warned you about the disturbance that your loose speech caused, and he doesn't want a repeat."

"That's right," Halbertson said, "If you cause any more ruckus, young man, you will be charged with contempt. And that will result in a trial in which you are the defendant, not just a witness."

Angus looked chastened, though he undercut it by leering at a single woman in the front row. She was probably twenty-two or -three, but looked smitten with him.

Herman said, "When you were accosted by the MacKay brothers did you have your hands inside her blouse?"

Every person in the room stopped breathing, and leaned forward in expectation of his answer.

Angus seemed to struggle with himself, as if he couldn't decide what to say.

"I remind you to only answer what I have asked."

"But I thought I was to tell the truth, the whole truth," said Angus.

"As indeed you shall, but only concerning the question asked."

Angus muttered something.

"Speak up," said Judge Halbertson.

"Yeah, my hands were under her blouse."

"No further questions, your honor."

The DeCosta kid was wonderful. He was so full of himself that he had antagonized the entire courtroom, save for a handful of hormonal women and girls. Herman was smiling, figuring he had the jury solidly on his side. The way he had presented it, they believed that Angus DeCosta had been ready to defile one of their children. It had only been providential that the MacKay brothers happened by at the right moment.

I rose to cross-examine the witness.

"So you were resting in the shade of the rhododendron, accompanied by Miss Palmer, when suddenly two young men accosted you. Are the two in this room, and if they are will you point to them?"

He took glee in using his crutch to identify Angus and Andrew MacKay. He couldn't have done better if I had coached him.

"Those are the bozos right there. They like to kill me, and I hadn't ever done them any harm."

I took him through the attack by the two MacKays. I had him display the bruises on his neck.

Angus and Andrew did some of my work for me by looking darts at DeCosta. Herman kept whispering to them, I am sure trying to moderate their behavior, but these were two undisciplined offspring of the town's most powerful family. They weren't used to being challenged.

"Did they threaten you with bodily harm?"

"Said they were gonna make me wish I was dead and then they were gonna grant my wish."

"Who said that, who threatened your life?"

He pointed his crutch at Angus MacKay. The MacKay boys squirmed in their seats. The court was quiet. The jury realized that this meant premeditation.

I took my time, sipped from my water glass, letting the point sink in. I walked back to the prosecutor's table and let my voice carry across the room.

"At any time did you threaten to harm the MacKay brothers?"

"I wished I coulda, but Andrew was too busy choking my neck for me to get a word out."

Andrew jumped to his feet. "That's a lie! You said you was gonna get your daddy's gun and blow my behind off!"

The usual uproar ensued, Halbertson gaveling, the bailiff pushing Andrew back into his seat, Herman shushing his clients, the MacKay clan growling and twitching in their seats at the insult offered their family. I moved as if to block the MacKay brothers from physically rushing DeCosta, though it was just histrionics.

"I wish to point out to the jury, that even if my client had said such a thing, it would not be a justification for attempted murder."

I skipped over the bit where he had bitten a chunk from the leg of his namesake cousin. We went through the events, letting DeCosta recount how the crowd of

MacKays separated the combatants, raining blows on him since he was at hand and their blood was up.

It was a pitiful story, one fifteen-year-old at the mercy of a mob, beaten mercilessly, thrown unconscious into the back of a pickup truck and then thrown off a bridge to drown. By the time I was done the jury looked grim and even the MacKay clan was subdued.

I turned my back on DeCosta and walked toward my table, as if I were done with him. He began to work the crutch under his arm in preparation to resume his seat in the wheelchair. I turned back as if I had forgotten something.

"One last question, Mr. DeCosta."

He settled back in his chair and looked confused.

"About Miss Palmer. When the MacKay brothers first accosted you, we know what you were doing. But what was she doing?"

His face lit up at the memory.

"She had her hands in my drawers, sir."

Judge Halbertson had to call another recess.

V.

In law, what plea so tainted and corrupt
But, being seasoned with a gracious voice,
Obscures the show of evil?
The Merchant of Venice
— *William Shakespeare*

THE TRIAL WAS going well. My assessment was that the town folk believed DeCosta had seduced the Palmer girl, as evidenced by the fact that she had her hands in his pants while his hands were under her blouse. Most of them felt that Angus had taken salacious and probably felonious advantage of a thirteen-year-old.

On the other hand I had planted the fact that the MacKays had threatened DeCosta's life. Once I established that the MacKay men had thrown him from the bridge, I had them for attempted murder. The jury would be compelled to convict, while the town would be certain that DeCosta had deserved every blow he received.

That was fine by me. I wanted the townsfolk to be up in arms when I got the conviction against Angus and Andrew MacKay.

The next witness was Mrs. Harmon, who went like a breeze, badmouthing the MacKay brothers almost nonstop, but also casting aspersions on the judge, the public defender, and the Presbyterian pastor alike. The jurors were as fascinated by her malicious gossip as her bizarre orange hair and overdone makeup. They reminded me of children looking through the glass wall of a roadside snake museum.

Jackie Sue Palmer followed Mrs. Harmon and she nearly brought the house down. The town had never before seen how brazen this hussy was. She was so full of herself I thought she was going to burst.

Her family sat in the upstairs gallery. The father looked stricken, while the mother alternated between pale fury and mauve anger. Jackie Sue's two siblings were having the time of their lives.

I confess I felt sympathy for her parents.

That girl must be a handful.

Although if she were a year or two older I might take her for a spin myself.

WHEN LUNCH RECESS came, I walked across the street in blazing sunlight, hoping to find Marshal Lawe at our town's diner. He was there, sipping a cherry cola, chatting with the proprietor, a high yella Negress who had fooled most of the town into thinking she was white.

My girlfriend, Suzy Ann, had recognized Gladys when she opened the diner. They had worked in the same bawdy house in New York. Suzy Ann was jealous that Gladys had been able to save her earnings and invest them.

It had been my first exposure to capitalist tendencies among whores. I had often wondered if they were going to unionize in the future.

I slid onto a swivel stool at the counter next to Lawe.

"You have a horse in this race?" I said.

"I don't follow you."

"I had a heckuva time finding enough jury members not related to Angus and Andrew MacKay. I thought you might have had something to do with that."

"I'm only the marshal, counselor. I've nothing to do with jury selection."

"I'm just trying to determine the lay of the land. This is an important case, and I think I have it all sewn up. The testimony is pretty clear."

Lawe didn't answer. He and I both knew why this case was important. It was to be the springboard for my senate campaign.

I tried again. "Is the public defender going to have any surprises for me, Marshal?"

He shook his head, neither confirming nor denying the possibility.

"I'm afraid the citizenry is going to be up in arms when the MacKay boys are convicted," I said.

"It's a sure thing, is it?" said Lawe. "Doesn't the jury still have to decide that?"

Gladys came around the counter with the judge's lunch on a foil-covered plate.

"Put this on the judge's tab, will ya?" said Lawe.

Gladys waved her hand in disgust. "Who you trying to fool, Icky? Hizz-onner never pays that tab."

"Icky?" I said.

Lawe spun on his heel and marched out, looking as if he wished Gladys had kept her mouth shut.

Gladys brought me my turkey on white. I have to admit the woman can build a pretty tasty sandwich.

"Do you think they'll be asking me to feed the jurors tonight, Mr. Sykes?" said Gladys.

"I doubt it. The jury will be instructed by the end of the afternoon, if it goes as I expect. The judge will send them all home for the night, and let them eat at their own expense, instead of the county's."

She hmmphed and wiped down the counters, then started refilling a saltshaker. I looked at her and thought I could perhaps add a little fuel to the coming fire.

"You might want to stay open late," I said. "More folks will be coming by for supper than usual. This kind of case draws a lot of people to town."

VI.

If you believe the theologians,
nothing is innocent.
— *Robert Gascoyne-Cecil*
Marquess of Salisbury

THERE WAS ONLY one surprise in the testimony of the afternoon, and Nick DeCosta occasioned it. Nick had a couple of contusions, but he was wearing a hundred dollar suit, better quality than either Herman's or mine. His shoes, hat, and necktie cost a month's salary. Coupled with his swarthy good looks, he was the picture of a successful Southern European immigrant.

But how had he come by this wealth? The public defender wanted to expose Nick as a moonshiner.

Because his goods tasted better and outsold the MacKay's brew, the MacKays already hated him. The remainder of the town folks who were not MacKay kin were staunch Prohibitionists.

This was doubly true of those in the Klan, it being a main tenet of their belief that alcohol was ruining the morals of the nation. DeCosta being Italian and Catholic was just icing on the cake. If Herman could get Nick to admit his occupation publicly he would earn the hatred of all factions in Potemkin County, helping dispose the jurors to acquit the MacKay boys.

However, it seemed that Mr. DeCosta had been to court before.

"Mr. DeCosta, you stated that you reside in Mills Gap. What do you do for a living?"

"I am the farmer."

"You're the best dressed farmer I've ever met," said Herman. "How do you afford such clothes?"

"Like the lily of the field."

"I don't understand."

"The lily of the field is like me. I do not toil or spin, but I have the beauty, yes?"

"You're a farmer, but you don't toil?"

"My English is not so perfect. I own the farm, I should say."

Herman was getting frustrated. He polished his glasses on his tie, then shook his finger in Nick's face.

"Do you or do you not make your income from selling moonshine?"

"A fifth."

"What?"

"A fifth. I take it."

There was a general hubbub as the jurors and the spectators tried to parse Nick's grammar and to make sense of his statement. Some were of the opinion that the fifth was a unit of alcoholic measure, others that he was referring to the fifth commandment.

That began a theological debate in the gallery. The Episcopalians held that the fifth commandment was "honor your father and mother," while the Lutherans said the fifth commandment was "thou shalt not kill."

Brother Franklin, a Baptist, had no opinion since he couldn't remember all ten, regardless of the order, though he was sure that moonshine was forbidden one way or another.

Judge Halbertson gave a ten-minute lecture on the constitution, the bill of rights, and the ability of a witness to shield himself from having to answer questions that might incriminate him.

Once the jurors and the town folk understood what taking the fifth meant, they were sure Nick was guilty as hell.

And he wasn't even on trial.

VII.

Justice is a temporary thing
that must at last come to an end.
On Marriage
— *Martin Luther*

AFTER THE JURY had been charged, I drove over to Suzy
Ann's. I needed to make a phone call but it couldn't be
from my office or anywhere I might be overheard.

Suzy Ann has a clientele wealthy enough to afford
the best. Her beaus demand good whiskey, clean sheets,
exotic favors, and access to a telephone. She has a nice two-
story house in the countryside. A line of poplars screen
the view from the highway, so that passersby cannot see
whose car is parked there.

Although the Ku Klux Klan claims that the Southern
European immigrants are polluting the country, I find
they bring certain charms with them. These dark-eyed,
dusky-skinned women are far more passionate than the
icy daughters of Albion.

Usually a little Puerto Rican gal answered the door,
but today Suzy Ann greeted me herself, wearing a filmy
dressing gown. With the light behind her in the doorway, I could see right through it. Some men claim she's
overweight, but I like a woman with a little meat on her.
It cushions the landing, so to speak. Plus it gave a nice

heft to her breasts, each of which was nearly the size of my head.

"I saw you coming up the driveway, Big Bill." She gave me a lascivious look. "Does Little Bill want to get wet today? You want some stinky on your dinky?"

"Save it for later, Sooie. I need to use the phone."

I pushed on past and took a seat at the little telephone table she had in the foyer. I took out a pocket humidor holding three high quality Cubans, some fine Bolivar Belicosos.

"Speaking of getting things wet, why don't you give these fellas your special treatment."

"You're ruining me for other men, Big Bill."

It sounded like a compliment, but she was scowling.

"You don't need to feed me a line, Sooie. I know for a fact I'm not that much larger than most men. It was one of my locker room discoveries when I played lacrosse at college."

She rolled her eyes. "That's not what I'm talking about. I can't keep treating your cigars that way. I'm losing all sensation down there."

"What do you mean?"

"I went to the doctor. He said I'm having an allergic reaction to the tobacco leaf. I'm getting all numb in my privates."

"That can't be possible," I said. "If you can't feel anything then why do you—well, bellow when you come?"

"For a college man you can be pretty thick."

"All right, educate me."

"Didn't I tell you I wanted to be on stage? I'm an actress."

I checked to make sure she wasn't pulling my leg.

"There's an extra sawbuck in it for you," I said.

She haggled a bit, and we settled on a rate that included letting me watch. She positioned herself on the divan directly across from me with her gown hiked up.

I picked up the phone as I watched. I dialed without having to use the operator, thanks to Suzy Ann having paid for a private line. She knew she couldn't keep her clientele with a party line, not in our puritanical county.

I got George on the phone. He was shift chief at the headquarters of the state militia and we had been at college together.

"George, don't say my name. Do you recognize my voice?"

"Of course. Why the rigmarole?"

"I've got a tip for you, but you can't say where it has come from. If anyone asks, say it was anonymous. There is going to be a Klan action tonight, out in Peony Springs."

"Action? Some kind of cross burning, torchlight parade and whatnot?"

"More likely a lynching."

"Why not tell the local police?"

"Because in this area, most of them belong to the KKK."

There was a pause while George considered the issue. When he spoke, it was with caution.

"I would think we should move out now, put a presence in the town, keep things from getting violent."

"You're not seeing the big picture, George. You know the Klan wants the Micks out of all state offices, and off the police forces, at least as captains," I said. "They don't like Catholics of any stripe."

"Where you going with this, Big—uh, where is this headed?"

"They're going to hang an Eye-Tie, a moonshiner. His son molested a local girl."

"I see," said George noncommittally.

"If you were to avenge the death of one of the mackerel snappers, it would do your career some good."

"What time is this going to take place?"

"There'll be a rally at half past eight."

"I better call out the men now and get them moving. It's three hours drive time."

"There's no point in just breaking up an illegal assembly. You need to quell a riot, arrest the murderers. Don't mobilize your men for another two hours."

I waited for a response, but I sensed George was wrestling with his conscience.

"Don't be a pissant," I said. "This is your chance to get the boys in Boston to take notice."

I hung up, not wanting to waste time arguing with him. Given two hours to stew, George would come to the right conclusion. I was satisfied my call had done its work.

"I'm going to spend the night here," I said.

"Alibis cost extra," said Suzy Ann.

She finished the third cigar and put it back in the humidor. She gave me a funny look as she handed it to me.

"So you're going to let them lynch Nick DeCosta?"

"You know Nick?" I left unspoken whether he was a client.

"He's been here a couple of times. Actually I have more problem keeping his kid away."

"That boy is going to have a jealous husband put a bullet in him before too long." I reached for one of my Bolivars, licked the tip, and fired it up.

There's nothing like the scent of woman admixed with fine Cuban leaf.

"But what you're doing ain't right," said Suzy Ann. "I thought you were an officer of the court."

"Look, I see myself as an altruist. I think this state would be better off if the Klan were extirpated once and for all."

"So would I. They're no friend of the working girl, though more than a few of them have been known to partake on occasion. Still, this is kind of raw."

"As long as they just march around burning crosses and roughing up the occasional colored boy, no one is going to take the time to do the job right. However, if they lynch a white man, and the state militia gets involved— Well, you can't make an omelet without breaking a few eggs, can you?"

"An altruist, huh? What's in it for the altruist?"

"By purging the state of this malignant cancer, the KKK, I become the most promising reform candidate for the next senate seat." I paused to puff the Belicosos. "Maybe I can ride it into the governor's mansion."

That got her interest. "You can't get elected governor without a wife. You're such an obvious Protestant and this is going to be a Catholic state soon."

I stared her down. "I doubt that marrying a Catholic whore would improve my chances."

"Watch your language, buster."

"I'll find someone suitable, don't you worry. And there will always be room in my bed for you."

Hell, if I choose the right spouse, there might be room for all three of us.

EULALA ALTBERGER SPOUT

In the choice of a horse and a wife, a man
must please himself, ignoring the opinion
and advice of friends.
> *Riding Recollections*
> — *G. J. Whyte-Melville*

I.

"EULALA! YOU HAVEN'T changed a bit."

Verna gave me that big gap-toothed smile I remembered so well.

"You're still as slim as when we worked at the mill, Verna."

I turned to Chestine, who had managed to put on twenty-five pounds or so, and took her hand. "I am so happy to see the two of you! Come in off the porch."

I had been surprised to get the letter from Verna, saying that she and my old workmate were taking a driving vacation. I hadn't heard from either of them in months.

We went inside and I made them some fresh squeezed lemonade. I showed them around the house and they ooh-ed and ah-ed about how lucky I was to live in such a beautiful place.

"What about the two of you?"

"We're renting a house together on Fillmore, about three blocks from the mill," said Chestine.

I thought about the close-minded mentality of the mill town. "That must save you money."

"Some, but it's a bunch of hooey that two can live as cheaply as one," said Chestine.

I didn't ask aloud what was being said about two

single women living together, but it must have shown on my face.

"People always find something to yap about," said Verna. "But we're quiet, we support the ladies auxiliary of the Rotary, and we've even joined the Friends of the Library."

I tried to figure out what wasn't being said. I soon gave it up.

"I was just about to make lunch. Would you two like potato salad with some fresh tomatoes on the side?"

JEDEDIAH CAME IN from the morning chores. He didn't seem too pleased to find company. He washed up and plopped himself in the easy chair in the living room, looking sullen. I offered him a glass of lemonade, which he took without a word of thanks.

Verna and Chestine made small talk with Jedediah, who grew more and more sour without any help from the citrus.

"Did you hear Mildred had triplets?" said Chestine. "Law, but that girl has her hands full now."

"I don't believe I've ever known anyone who had three at once," I called from the kitchen. "She had the two already, didn't she?"

"Who's Mildred?" said Jedediah.

"Oh, I've told you about her, Jed. We worked the same line at the mill," I said. "She was my supervisor back then, before she married Earl."

"And it's driving Earl to distraction," said Verna. "He's threatening to move out until the kids are housebroken and they stop their howling."

"Who's Earl?" said Jed in a grim tone. "He work at the factory, too?"

Chestine laughed at his expression. "Don't fret so. Eulala never gave him a second glance. She was so stuck on you, and always planning how the two of you were going to buy this farm and all, once she'd saved enough for the down payment."

I saw Jedediah scowl and knew she had touched a sore point. Why did Chestine have to bring that up? Earl was sensitive about the money I had saved to buy our farm, though he had no call to be. It was just his pride, the way men get. Not that Chestine would know anything about that.

I diverted his attention by pointing out the window. "That's a fine car you two drove up in."

Jedediah stared at it, long and hard.

Verna was all too pleased that I had noticed. "I just love the Oldsmobile. We've only had it three months, but it sure runs like a dream."

"Smooth riding, too," said Chestine. "Some of the roads out this way are pretty rough."

"Is that because there isn't the tax base for road maintenance in the rural part of the county?" said Verna.

"Let's not talk politics in mixed company, *ladies*," said Jedediah, embarrassing me by his emphasis on the last word. Jedediah always was a good Bible man.

"You'll have to excuse Jed, girls," I said. "He's old fashioned that way."

"You know," said Chestine, addressing Jedediah, "women do have the vote now."

Jedediah wrinkled his nose like someone had passed gas.

"I can barely afford to keep my Ford pickup running," said Jedediah, ignoring her. "That Oldsmobile's an expensive car, especially for a woman."

"Chestine's been promoted to line supervisor," said Verna. "That helped quite a bit."

"And Verna makes half the payments," said Chestine.

I saw Jedediah's eyebrows shoot up toward his hairline. I relieved the tension by calling them all to the table. We had some desultory talk of the weather and the crops Jed and I grew. I thought things had calmed down.

"We read about the attempted murder case that's gone to trial," said Verna. "That must be plenty exciting in a quiet town like this."

Jedediah's eyes narrowed and I could see he was getting hot under the collar.

"It's made the papers all across the state," said Chestine. "People are watching to see how the case is handled, what with there being sexual molestation, and a half-Italian involved."

"Feelings are running high about the case," said Verna.

"Of course they're running high," said Jedediah. "It shows the damn immigrants are out of control, coming into our country, taking jobs from decent folk, raping our daughters—"

"Jedediah! I'll thank you not to use that kind of language in front of ladies."

Jedediah gave me a hard look, then threw his napkin down atop his half-finished lunch.

Chestine gave him a chiding look. "You're not going to finish Eulala's delicious potato salad? 'Today you don't know where to put a bit, tomorrow you won't know where to get a bit.' That's what my granny always said."

He backed away from the table, got his hat from the hook by the door, and raised his shoulder for me to follow him out to the front porch.

Verna and Chestine gave each other knowing glances as I followed him outside.

II.

> We would often be sorry,
> if our wishes were gratified.
> *The Old Man and Death*
> — *Aesop*

"I WANT THOSE two biddies gone from my home when I return."

"When you return?" I said. "You mean from afternoon chores?"

He shook his head. "I have an errand in town. I should be back within a couple of hours. Make sure they've left. And also make sure they know they are not welcome to visit ever again."

"These are my friends, not yours. They didn't come to visit you."

"Well, it's my house and I don't want witches like that using up my air."

"You've no call to act like this, Jedediah. I've few enough friends as it is. We never go any place together, and you're out night after night seeing those terrible Klansmen, doing I don't know what."

He reached over and slapped me across the face.

"Don't question my actions, woman. Just make sure that they are out of here before I get back, or there'll be hell to pay. Do you understand me?"

I said nothing, just held my throbbing face.

"I said, do you understand me?" He raised his hand again. "Or do you require further instruction?"

"I understand you."

He stared at me hard, waiting.

Oh my lord, he's going to make me.

"I understand you, *dear*," I said, trembling.

His lips stretched thin in satisfaction. He turned abruptly and began walking the road to town.

I stayed in the shade on the porch, trying to regain my composure.

LIKE MANY WOMEN of Potemkin County I had finished high school with no particular skills to offer the marketplace. I was not inclined to typing or dictation. I had worked as a waitress part time in the summer of my junior year and hated it. I didn't want to repeat the experience.

My parents had recently given up their small farm back then. I missed it terribly. Mom and Pop had taken up clerking at the bank and I couldn't imagine why they had traded the fields for the confines of the city. They answered that I didn't know what a difficult proposition the farming life was.

I met Jedediah at a church social. We hit it off and it was such a relief to have a steady beau. He was five years older than me and had been working as a farmhand in the eastern reach of Pennsylvania. He hadn't managed to save much, but he loved farm life. When his mother came down with the tuberculosis, he'd moved back to Peony Springs and had taken work in the hardware store.

We sparked a bit and I began to have dreams of a

wedding, though I didn't see how we would afford anything more than a one-room walk-up to live in. Neither
of us thought much of that idea.

I heard there was plenty of work in the mills
downriver, and I thought I might take a job for a year
and build a savings account. I've never been sure who
first suggested this idea, but even if it was Jedediah I
certainly fell in with it right away. Anything to get out of
Peony Springs. Since my parents had given up the farm
,I didn't care for living in one half of the side-by-side we
rented in town.

Jedediah and I agreed I'd work there for only a year,
and we'd each save as hard as we could. He'd look for
a farm of any size that might sustain a family (oh, how
I blushed at the thought!) and once we had the down
payment we'd get married.

Jedediah came up twice that year, once on the Fourth
of July and again at Thanksgiving. It was on that second
visit that he announced he had found the place for
us. I squealed with delight, but he soon put a damper
on that.

He'd been doing some research, he said, and we
needed more to get started than we had thought. Cash
money would be needed for seed and livestock and even
more to buy some used machinery.

He gave me a handwritten list where he'd calculated
the cost of each item to set up our farm. I realized he was
telling me, though not in so many words, that I'd have to
work the mill at least two more years.

IT WAS RIGHT after that following New Year that
Earl Hickam had asked me out. He was the shift

supervisor and he was always on the prowl, dating and taking advantage of new girls on the line.

I didn't want to date him, but I didn't want trouble either. To deflect his attention I gushed about the man I was engaged to back home.

"Engaged? I don't see any ring on your finger."

I reddened. "Jedediah is saving up for one that's just right."

"You got no ring, it's not real nor even serious. You're still allowed to date."

"Well, I'm serious about it. And I don't date other men."

He pulled a clipboard from the wall and pretended to study it.

"I guess that's all right, anyhow. I didn't realize you were scheduled on the night shift."

"I'm not on the night shift."

"Yep, scheduled on the night shift from now on," he said, and paused. "Of course, if I were dating a gal on the night shift, she'd probably get changed back to a day schedule so we could go out."

I gave him a bleak glare. "My break's over. I need to get back to the line, Earl."

"I find the workplace runs more smoothly if the line workers address me as Mr. Hickam."

Word spread about the incident, because there had been other girls within earshot. That was when I was approached by Verna and Chestine for the first time. They commiserated with me over my treatment by the boss. I blubbered about how I felt dirty because of his suggestions and wondered how I was going to face my fiancé.

They told me to come to a program that night. There was a committee to unionize the workers of the mill. I didn't really understand what they were talking about, but I sure needed some friends at that point.

That was the beginning of my union period. There was an inordinate number of meetings needed to get us organized, and then a vote by the members to formally incorporate the union. At long last the union presented the management of the mill with a list of demands to improve working conditions.

We all had agreed that we'd leave wage demands until later. We'd show some backbone first by making the workplace safer.

III.

> Perhaps there is no happiness in life
> so perfect as the martyr's.
> *The Trimmed Lamp*
> —O. Henry

AT LAST I could delay no longer and went back inside. Chestine and Verna sat without a word, staring at my face, which I imagine must have had his dark handprint on my left cheek.

If they knew this much, it didn't matter what else they knew.

I got things off my chest that I had been holding in for five years.

They were good listeners. They let me speak until I had no more to say.

"It's a crying shame the way that man treats you," said Verna. "I don't know why you don't throw him out. Surely the court would side with you when there's physical abuse."

"Don't be naïve, Verna," said Chestine. "We live in a bourgeois patriarchy."

"Besides, Jedediah is drinking buddies with most of the police in this town," I said. "He and the judge are both in Kiwanis. And half the town is in the Klan and Jed is the Kleagle."

"What's a Kleagle?" said Chestine.

"It means he's a big shot among those drips," I said.

"But still, the law ought to protect a woman if her husband does her harm."

I waved that remark aside. "I'm mortified to admit this," I said, "but he'd be better off without me. He'd get the whole farm."

"You worked three years to earn that down payment," said Chestine.

"But when the deed was drawn it was only in his name. He said it didn't sit right with him not to be the owner. And back then I was crazy in love."

"Just crazy sounds more like it," said Verna.

"No need to be so mean," said Chestine.

"Of course now that we're behind on the mortgage, maybe it's not the big deal it once was."

"Those bastard bankers always squeeze the little guy," said Verna.

"And then we never had any children," I said.

"Miscarriages?"

"I didn't get pregnant at all. I think he's the one with the barrenness, but I suppose it could be me just as easily."

"What does your doctor say? I mean, he can tell whose fault it is, can't he?"

"Only if Jedediah would allow him to test."

We sat in tense silence as the sun dipped, sending shafts of honey-colored light across the living room, dust motes dancing in the air like black fireflies.

"Well, it's just another example of the exploitation of the proletariat by capital," said Chestine. She'd always been big on Marxist theories of labor. It helped her rise in the union, but she'd been careful not to side too closely

—161—

with the communists. Even so, she had the tendency, you could see it in her.

"It's hard to see how I am a worker toiling in a factory I don't own, making products I can't afford," I said.

"I mean in principle," said Chestine. "You know, oppression of the person who actually produces the wealth. That's you. Big capital fat cats getting rich off the sweat of the worker. That's Jed. Or maybe the bank."

"Actually part of the reason we came to visit was to see if you would be interested in setting up a cell," said Verna.

Chestine corrected her tersely. "Not a cell. A co-op, a farmer's co-operative."

They went on for some time about co-operatives and collectives and socialization of farms. And then some more about the coming revolution and the workers throwing off their chains. And even more about property being theft and how commercial capital was a system of plunder.

I listened as long as I could. Then I filled them in on the realities of life among rural farmers. Jefferson's ideals and the small farm freeholder. And mostly how the Klan was on the lookout for anything that smelled of Bolshevism. Then I reminded them that my husband was head of the Klan in this area.

Not that I agreed with him, I said. I was just trying to let them know how people believed in this county.

Soon enough they realized their missionary work was of no use.

IV.

The proletarians have nothing to lose
but their chains.
The Communicst Manifesto
— *Karl Marx and Friedrich Engels*

I PACKED A picnic dinner for the gals, and told them of a
nice park about an hour's drive toward their town. They
wanted to be on the road and reach home before it was
dark. I wished I were going with them, almost wished I
still had a job back at the mill.

It was on the tip of my tongue to ask if they might get
me back on the line. In hindsight that six dollars a week
seemed mighty sweet. Jedediah and I had been struggling
to keep up the mortgage payments on this farm. On the
other hand, I liked the way I could set my own schedule
here in Potemkin. And of course, leaving your husband
is morally wrong. It's a wife's duty to submit to the man
of the house.

I was puzzled by something. I knew Verna and Chestine had but one day off per week. If you were absent from
the mill two days in a row it was likely that somebody took
your place on the line and you wouldn't get it back.

"This isn't your day off, so how did you get here on a
Thursday?" I said to Chestine.

"The year after you left the union won the right to vacations for us," she said.

"Today's not a holiday."

"Not holidays," said Verna. "After you've been working five years you're entitled to a week off without losing your job."

I couldn't believe my ears. "You mean they pay you *not* to work for a week?"

Chestine turned red about the ears. "No. You don't get paid. You just get to take the week off."

"You two can afford to take a week off without pay? How many of the other gals do this?"

"Not many. It was less of a concession than the union thought it would be."

"Next contract negotiation we plan to bargain for paid vacations," said Verna. "Unpaid vacation time was getting our foot in the door."

I shook my head in amazement. "You two are plan-ahead thinkers, that's for sure."

I put chicken, potato salad, pickles, and a quart jar of lemonade into a cardboard box. I put in two of my chipped dishes and a couple of old coffee mugs along with forks as well.

"You can't just give us those utensils and plates, Eulala."

"You're right."

"Let us pay you for them."

"I have something better in mind. This way you have a reason to come on back and return them. Or maybe I'll come and visit you to pick them up."

Verna looked dubious. "You think Jedediah would let you visit us in the city?"

They knew better. I had nothing to say so I picked up the box and went outside.

Verna and Chestine showed me their car. It was a real beauty and the interior was luxurious. I was envious that the two of them could afford such a magnificent machine. It gave them the freedom to travel the country at a moment's notice.

I thought about asking them if they still thought property was theft, but decided I didn't have time for that discussion. Besides I was glad they had come by to see me and I didn't want to poison that particular well.

I hadn't realized how lonely I was for some female companionship, and how little of it I had. Jedediah had managed to drive off most of the women I liked, and I was left with only those he approved of. Mostly Klanswomen, mousey as all get out, not a live wire in the bunch.

We hugged and kissed and promised each other we'd stay in touch. I waved and waved and their dust plume was still visible when a hand touched my shoulder from behind. I took a fright and turned around.

V.

> ...Lo! With a little rod
> I did but touch the honey of romance—
> *Hélas*
> — *Oscar Wilde*

IT WAS ONLY James Scott, the big Appalachian dummy that Jedediah used to do his heavy lifting.

"You almost gave me heart failure, James."

"I'm sorry, Mrs. Spout. I had word I was to meet Jedediah here."

"He's not here right now."

James just stood there, unsure of what he should do next. He looked pitiful in the afternoon sun.

"You want to come inside, get out of the heat and have something cool to drink?"

He thought that one over for about twelve seconds and reached a conclusion.

"Nope. That wouldn't be right, being as how Jed's not here."

"How about if you just sit in the shade under this elm? I can bring you somewhat."

He thought long again.

"I guess that'd be all right."

He took a seat and I went inside. When I brought him

his glass I could see he had a question. I waited for him to get it out.

"Are you going with us tonight, Mrs. Spout?"

"What do you mean, James?"

Panic spread across his stolid features.

"I shouldn't have said nothing, Mrs. Spout. Just forget about it. I didn't mean nothing by it. I'm just here to meet Jedediah. We aren't planning a thing, not a thing."

I cut him off or he would have babbled on till dark.

"You and the Klan got something going on?"

"No, no, not the Klan, no sirree, not the Knights."

"You sure now?"

He nodded with such vigor I feared his head might come loose at the root.

"So it's just you and Jedediah going out tonight?" I said.

"Well, uh." He stumbled for a moment, but knew he had to answer. "Yep."

"Where are *just* the *two* of you going? It wouldn't be a certain settlement down by the county line, would it?"

"Darktown? Nope, that's not it." Now he seemed to be genuinely confused. "I don't think so."

"Is it the Knights, then? You and the other kluxers up to no good? Bunch of boys playing ghost, scaring folks. Don't you know it's too early for Halloween?"

"You've got no call to talk like that, Mrs. Spout. The Klan has a noble purpose, to protect the purity of our women, to prevent the mixing of the white race with the trash people—"

"Oh, please. You don't have to prevent something that ain't happening."

James lapsed into silence and stared at something

behind me. I turned and saw Jedediah striding up the road from town.

"Eulala, why'd you leave James sitting outside?"

He appeared light-hearted and I confess I was surprised.

"I didn't want to go in, Jedediah," said James. "Didn't think it was proper."

That removed any light-heartedness from Jed's expression.

"Not proper? What'd she do to make you feel that way?" He turned to me, frowning. "What did you say to him, girl?"

"Nothing like that, Jed." I said. "Do you want a glass of ice water? You must be hot after that walk."

He looked from me to James and back.

"James, you wait here a bit. I need to have a chat with the little woman while she gets me that drink."

Once we were inside I turned to him and hissed, "You think I don't know what's going on?"

He appeared to be amused at what I said. "Let's hear it. What do you think is going on?"

"You and James are heading down to Darktown, listen to that jazz, and get drunk."

"Shows what you know. We're fixing to march against the injustice about to be done to the MacKay boys."

This caught me off guard.

"Well, if that's what it is, then I'd like to come along. I believe we see eye to eye on this matter."

"Politics is the business of men. You're staying home."

"So no other women will be there?" He blinked at that. I knew that plenty of the Klan wives attended all the functions. "Business of men, huh? That sounds more like monkey business to me."

I could see anger begin to cloud up in his face, but I was working myself up pretty good, too.

"You think I don't know about your floozies? Well, I do. I know you've got a dusky-skinned whore down in Darktown. You ever think maybe you picked up a disease from her and that's why we never had children? Them social diseases do that, you know. I read about it. You get some kind of scar inside your pecker—"

I didn't even see him cock his fist.

VI.

No more tears now;
I will think about revenge.
— *Mary, Queen of Scots*

IT WAS NEAR nine o'clock when I came to. I lay sprawled on the living room rug, soaking in a puddle of my own pee. When I tried to sit up the room swam around me and I retched up my lunch. The lemonade didn't help matters and I thought the mix of bile and citrus was going to burn out my throat.

I crawled to the kitchen sink and pulled myself upright, running cold water over my face and gulping it down until I began to feel the pain in my jaw. In the bedroom I changed into a clean housedress and I caught sight of myself in the mirror over the dresser. I tried to sob, but that hurt too much, so I was restricted to muffled whimpers.

It looked like he'd broken my jaw. For certain he'd knocked out a tooth. I couldn't find my molar on the floor so I figured I must have swallowed it while I was unconscious. My face was swoll to the size of a volleyball, my left eye was black, and my lip was puffed. I couldn't recognize myself.

This was the last straw. I was going to punch his ticket

for good. I slammed open the closet to get his rifle. It was gone, the box of shells, too.

He must have it with him.

I stormed about the bedroom, jerking out drawers, piling his clothes in a heap. All that exercise made the blood begin to flow and my head ached something fierce. I stopped and ran the cold water across my face again while I tried to decide what to do.

I got out a stepladder and pushed open the little door that opens into the attic space. I had a trunk up there where I had collected all the things for when I would have a baby. I pulled it down and went through it, my tears now being more for the child I would never have and less for the mess he had made of my face.

There. I knew it was in here.

I pulled out the slingshot my daddy had made from the branch crotch of a yew tree. He said every child needed himself a sling shot, and he figured I had lost mine sometime back. There was a bag of marbles in there, too. I took them both out and put the rubber on the sling.

As a girl I had been a tomboy when it came to potting squirrels. I looked around the room. I needed to see if I still had the touch.

Yes. I always hated that photo of his shifty-eyed father.

I let loose and the glass over the photo shattered. I bent and checked the picture. I had been aiming for the eye, but I had hit Daddy Spout in the mouth.

I spent the next thirty minutes getting my aim back, meanwhile relieving the house of some of its worst ornaments. His mother's china. His high school football trophy. That horrible painting of a sunset. I felt much better for it.

And then I began to vomit. I guess I had swallowed a great deal of blood, though it looked more like black rice coming up. The smell made me gag long after my stomach was empty.

Yep. There's my tooth.

It made me realize that he had to pay for this.

I put the full bag of marbles in the pocket on my dress along with the slingshot and marched toward town.

I SAW THE first casualties about a quarter of a mile outside of Peony Springs. Mrs. Bates and her son Willy were holding each other up. Blood dripped off the end of Mrs. Bates' nose.

I stared at them and they stared back. I gathered they didn't recognize me.

"Jenny, it's me. Eulala."

Her hand flew to her mouth and she gasped in alarm.

"Oh, my gawd. You, too?"

She tugged on her son's arm and hurried away before I could ask what had happened.

After meeting six more women and four children, all bloodied or bruised, I had put together most of the story.

"So, the state militia came in to break up the Klan march?" I said to Margaret Hambley, a girl I used to sit behind in tenth grade. The way she looked at me I thought she hadn't understood what I said. I was having a hard time talking around the swelling and bruises both inside and outside my mouth.

"March? I thought you were there."

"Where?"

"The lynching. That's when the militia showed up."

"A lynching!" I would not have believed my neighbors capable of it. I thought that such things occured only in the deep south, not New England.

"If the militia didn't bloody your face with their billy clubs, what happened to you?" said Margaret.

"Jedediah," I blurted out. I hadn't planned to tell anyone of my abuse at his hands, but seeing all these others injured had somehow changed that.

Margaret gave a small tight smile. "Can't say I'm surprised. There's been plenty of talk about his temper. He beat up that Darcy girl while you were working down at the mill."

"Darcy?" This was the first I had heard of her.

"You must have known. He was going out with her while you were gone. I mean it was all over town." She gave another of those horrible smiles. "We all felt so sorry for you. We couldn't believe how forgiving you were to go ahead with the marriage anyway."

I was so humiliated I couldn't speak any further and brushed past her. At the city jail, I saw half a dozen militiamen milling about the broken entry. I sidled over to the shadows where my damaged face wasn't visible and tapped Claude Hoffman, our town's sixty-year-old apothecary, on the arm.

"What's this about?"

"The state boys are making sure the MacKay brothers don't take this opportunity to escape."

"Looks like it was broken from the outside going in, not someone trying to get out. Who broke down the door?"

He gave me a strange look.

"From all accounts it was your husband Jedediah, with some help from James Scott."

"Oh," I said, taken aback. "Do you know where he is? Did the militia arrest him?"

He shook his head. "No one's seen him for the better part of two hours, out in the for—"

He broke off, not wanting to say it out loud.

"At the lynching?" I said.

"He never came out of the woods."

I turned to go.

"Wait," said Claude. "I don't think the woods are a safe place for a lady tonight."

"I need to find him."

Claude nodded his approval. "You always were a loyal one. And Jedediah may need your help."

Claude can think whatever he wants.

I skirted the militia and made my way into the woods.

THE BEASTS

The beast of many heads,
the staggering multitude.
  The Malcontent
      — Marston and Webster

I.

CHIEF LIE IN shade, rest by Judge den. Chief not like Judge. Judge mean, smell like bad fruit. Bad fruit no good, no. Meat good, bread good.

Judge not finish food middle of day. Judge drink bad fruit, put plate outside door with food still on. Food good, Chief eat later. Chief not kill Judge today, heh, heh. Maybe tomorrow, heh, heh.

Man-bitch come to Judge's den. She look at Chief with fear. Good. She hit door, Judge bark from inside den, she go inside. Chief lie in shade, watch. Will food come?

Inside Judge den, man-bitch bark. Loud sounds, Chief listen.

Trouble? Chief kill man-bitch, kill Judge? Chief stand up, show angry teeth.

Master come, call Chief. Say, "Good dog, Chief. Sit, boy." Pat on head, give food.

Master smart, not stay in room full of man and man-bitches like Judge. Master good, smell right. Say, "Good boy. Shake. Sit. Nice dog." Give Chief treat. Master not like Judge, Master good.

Master carry food to Judge den, not hit door. Master listen by door. Man-bitch come out, Judge bark again. Master set food down by door, talk to man-bitch. Master not watch Chief. Chief watch food, guard food.

Chief see Kaw on top of Judge den. Kaw eyes bright, dead mouse in mouth. Chief can smell mouse. Where Kaw get dead mouse? Chief want Kaw go away.

Kaw look at Chief, swallow mouse. Kaw say, "Kaaaaa kaaaaaaaaw." Kaw look at Chief again, bad look. Chief angry.

Master take man-bitch to shade. Master talk, no see Kaw. Man-bitch no hear Kaw.

Kaw look at food by Judge den. Kaw hop to ground, look at Chief. Chief pretend not see Kaw. Kaw hop close to food. Bad Kaw. Kaw want Judge food. Kaw hop again.

Chief jump at Kaw and bark. Kaw fly away fast, too fast for Chief. Chief know Kaw fly to cornfield at edge of Chief's territory.

Chief not kill Kaw today, maybe tomorrow, grrrrr. Chief show angry teeth, but Kaw gone. Chief mark territory by Judge door.

Master call Chief. "Here, boy. Something, something. Come, boy."

Chief walk to Master, look at Master, look at man-bitch. Master pat Chief. "Good boy."

Master give Chief food? Treat? No treat. Why?

Master show Chief to man-bitch. Chief sniff her crotch, not sniff her before. Now Chief remember man-bitch always.

Chief sniff again. Not her time, not ready for mating. She pat on head, and push nose away. She afraid. Good, not kill man-bitch today, heh, heh.

Master say, "Chief, something, something, something. Chief guard."

Chief like to guard, good at guard. Chief lick Master's hand. Master show happy teeth. Chief look at man-bitch, sniff crotch again. Man-bitch have more fear, and something else. She look at Master. Maybe ready to mate soon?

Chief look at Master. He not know this about man-bitch, but show happy teeth to her anyway. She show happy teeth. Why they not mate now? Master take her to den under ground, down stairs. Den good for mating, maybe they mate now? No. Talk, talk, talk, no mate.

Master say to Chief, "Sit, boy. Guard. No barking, Chief. Stay." Why? Master leave, Chief stay. Where Master go?

Man-bitch go into room, take off outer skin. Go to other room, make water. Smell not bad, not good, she not sick. Chief sniff her again, she say, "No, Chief. Bad dog."

Chief not bad dog, Chief good dog, sniff her more. She push head, she not strong. Chief strong, not move head. She afraid. Good, not kill her now, heh, heh. Maybe tomorrow.

Master come back, bring food to man-bitch. No bring food to Chief. Why? Is Chief bad dog? Master scratch Chief head, talk to man-bitch. Master look at Chief, say, "Come, boy."

Chief walk with Master, up stairs. Master say, "Down, boy. Guard. Something, something, something, later. Good dog." Master show Chief happy teeth, but not happy. Why Master not happy? Maybe Master think of Kaw? Chief hate Kaw.

Chief lie down in shade, guard man-bitch. Chief good dog, get food, get pat later. Why later, why not now?

Chief think of Kaw, Kaw bad. Kaw think Kaw is Master of all. Kaw wrong, even Master is not Master of all. Master is Master of some things, not all.

Master is Master of Chief, good thing. Master good, Chief good, Kaw bad.

Chief kill Kaw, tomorrow, heh, heh.

Chief lie in shade. Nothing come, nothing move. Chief hot.

Chief sleep.

II. Kleagle Jedediah Spout

I HAD BUSINESS at the courthouse. Couldn't afford to
be seen, for certain not by Lawe, and I hate being out
in the heat. Still, I had to get a message to Bill Sykes,
and it wasn't a note I wanted in the wrong hands. So
there I was, walking in the shadows along Main Street,
cutting into the alley behind the diner, rapping at the back
entry, the smell of yesterday's plate scrapings thick in my
nostrils.

A colored dishwasher opened the door, drying a plate
on his apron. I was surprised, but not pleased. *Taking jobs
from real Americans.* This was the kind of thing my klavern
would put an end to, the reason I had been elevated to
Kleagle.

"You the new pearl diver?" I said. "What happened
to Hauptman?"

The dishwasher averted his eyes. "Don't know any
Hauptman, suh."

I was about to fry, standing there in the sun, but wasn't
sure I wanted to share the humid service area with the
darkie help. "Can you ask Miss Gladys to come back and
see me? Tell her it's…" I trailed off, not sure I wanted to
reveal my name to some transient.

Something flashed in the dishwasher's eyes. "Sure
thing, Mr. Spout." He paused a beat, lowered his eyes

again. "I recognized you right off, suh." He faded back into the dim interior.

I moved into a shadow cast by a telephone pole. Wondered how I was known by sight to a dishwasher I'd never met.

Maybe the Secret Empire isn't as secret as I think.

Gladys came out, looked around to see if we were alone, fixed her good eye on me. "How can I help you, Mr. Spout?"

"I need to get a note to Bill Sykes."

Gladys looked unhappy, like maybe she wanted to say something smart, couldn't stop herself. "I don't see how that's my business. I run a diner, not a postal service."

I gave her my glare, the one that always shuts them up. "I'm trying to do you a favor, Gladys. And you're going to do one for me."

She held her tongue then, though I could see she was fighting to control herself.

"Don't you usually take a gallon of punch over to the courtroom in the heat of the afternoon?" I said. "Make sure that Sykes gets this note. Don't make it obvious, slip it to him."

I put a folded square of paper into her hand. She flinched just a little when my skin touched hers, and that was just fine. Better she be righteously afraid of the Knights, much better.

I saw her get her gumption up and she said, "I thought you were doing me a favor in return."

"Stay open late. You can do a lot of business tonight after dark."

Her face clouded over. "What are your boys up to?"

I ignored her question. "I'd recommend your new dish-washer take the evening off. This has nothing to do with him, no reason for him to get hurt in the confusion."

She clenched her fist and began to tremble. I took that as a sign my work was done for now. Turned on my heel and set off down the alley, heading for a shortcut to the creek.

I was some ten yards away when I heard her speak out.

"You're not the law, Mr. Spout."

I spun around, ran back, and backed her up against the wall hard. Her breathing came hard and jerky when I leaned into her face.

Whispered in her ear, "We're talking about God's law, Gladys. You'd best not forget it."

III. Chief

CHIEF SLEEP, DREAM. Dream of long ago time, before Chief a pup, before Chief mother a pup, when animals talk. No mans, no Masters. Only the pack.

Pack Leader strongest dog, smartest dog.

Pack Leader bay at moon, call to pack. Pack come and sit. Pack Leader say, "Time to hunt, hunt deer tonight. Kill many deer, all dogs eat, all dogs happy."

Dogs like to hunt, dogs show happy teeth.

Dogs hear wolfs howl from mountain top. Bitches worry, one bitch say, "Pups not run fast. Who watch pups?"

Pack Leader say, "Great Dog in Sky watch pups, pups safe."

Bitch not happy, show angry teeth. Pack leader nip bitch, she yelp, she lie on back. Pack Leader say, "Grrrrr. Hunt now."

All dogs run into night, pack run fast like wind. Pups not run fast, pups behind.

Pack Leader find scent of deers, call for all dogs follow. Into forest, dark, smell deer fear. Pack is happy, pack run fast-fast. Deers afraid, run fast-fast. Pups far behind.

Now Chief dream of coons. Coons hear dogs bark, coons afraid. Coons clever, climb trees, make no sound, Pack run by below. King Coon watch dogs go by.

Some dogs smell coons, stop, bark at trees. Pack Leader

growl, come back, show angry teeth, say, "Grrrrr. Dogs hunt deers now, hunt coons tomorrow."

King Coon watch dogs run after deer. Dogs gone, coons happy, coons safe. King Coon not happy. King Coon angry, climb down tree, look for danger, see dog pups come. King Coon angry-angry.

Pups see King Coon, show angry teeth to King Coon, bite at coon. Pups small, King Coon bite at pup, kill one pup, tear apart, other pups afraid. King Coon call other coons from tree, surround pups.

One coon say, "Kill all pups? Eat?"

King Coon clever. Think, say. "No kill, bring pups, follow."

Coons show teeth to pups, pups afraid. In dream Chief afraid, Chief whimper.

Coons take pups into dark forest, take far, find cave. Smell fire, smell two-legs.

Coons afraid. One coon say, "King, go back? Now? Two-legs bad, fire bad."

King Coon show teeth. Angry? Happy? Not know. King Coon say, "Take pups to cave, leave pups for two-legs. Two-legs eat pups, make dogs angry, dogs and two-legs fight, kill. Only coons left in forest."

Coons happy, say, "King smart. King good." Coons take pups to two-leg cave.

Two-legs come, see pups, kill pups, eat pups. In dream Chief sad, cry.

One small two-leg not eat pup. Hold pup, pup afraid. Small two-leg talk soft to pup, "Good pup. Safe. Stay." Small two-leg give food to pup, pup eat. Pup lick two-leg hand. Two-leg show happy teeth, love pup.

Pup love two-leg.

In dream Chief see pup grow to dog, small two-leg

grow to Master, longtime-longtime. Master name dog, call dog Little Bear. Little Bear happy, Master happy. Master and Little Bear hunt, hunt deer, hunt coons, kill deers, eat deers.

Little Bear hate coons, kill coons when catch. Not eat coon, tear apart, angry-angry.

Master take coon from Little Bear. Little Bear show angry teeth. Master hit Little Bear. Little Bear yelp, put ears down, put tail down, lie on ground.

Master take coon, burn with fire, feed Little Bear. Little Bear look at Master, eat burned coon. Master show happy teeth to Little Bear. Little Bear lick Master hand.

Longtime-longtime Master and Little Bear hunt in forest, hunt porcupine, hunt coons, hunt rats. No food, Master no eat, Little Bear no eat, night come. Master and Little Bear sleep hollow log.

Pack come in night. Little Bear look from log and watch.

Pack Leader howl, call to pack. "Great Hunt this night, hunt forever. Hunt deers into sky, see Great Dog in Sky. Pack live forever."

Master hear, not understand Pack Leader. Little Bear listen, understand.

Little Bear want Great Hunt, stick nose out of log. Pack run by, fast-fast, not see Little Bear. Little Bear see pack going. Little Bear go, leave Master?

Master afraid many dogs, hide in log.

Little Bear look at pack. Little Bear look at Master long time.

In sleep Chief whine.

IV. Kaw

I WATCHED THE Barker from the tree-with-wires-not-leaves. The Bright-Eye-in-the-Sky was gone, but the sky was not dark. Mist moved from the trees at the edge of town, of town.

I saw the Barker twitch in his sleep. The Barker chased dream-rabbits. The Barker is stupid. There is still food on plate by the door. The Barker did not eat it, so I will eat it, eat it.

I flew to the roof. I looked at the food. I looked at the Barker. Was he pretending sleep? I was nervous. I looked at the Barker again. No, the Barker was asleep, asleep.

I hopped to the ground. Would the Barker wake up? Would the Barker bite at Kaw? No, the Barker slept. Stupid Barker. I am smarter than the Barker. All Kaws are smarter than Barkers. Why did the Bright-Eye make such stupid creatures, creatures?

I walked to the food. I looked at the Barker again. Nothing. I looked at the door. No movement. I look at the food. I took a bite in my beak, held it up in the air, looked left, looked right. No one moved.

I swallowed. I was happy, so happy I almost said "Kaaaaw." But I kept quiet. I ate the food, the food.

When the food was gone, I preened my feathers. I am so smart, eating right next to the stupid Barker. I hopped closer to the Barker. I looked at the Barker's closed eye. I saw his eye move beneath the lid. I hopped back. Would the Barker wake up? No, no.

I walked proudly right next to the Barker, watching its eye move. So, the Barker dreamed again, and now it whimpered in its sleep, its sleep.

Maybe I will peck out the Barker's eye. Yes, peck out the eye of the stupid Barker. The Barker would be blind and the Kaw would be master of the town, the town.

"Kaaaaaaaaw!"

V. Kleagle

A MIST HAD come in off the marsh as the sun set and the temperature dropped. That was jake with me, as it might cover the movement of my men into town. And it was a sight better than the heat of the day. My spirits began to revive.

This was a good night for it, time for the Klan to assert itself, set to right some of the blasphemy these Italians and other Catholics had brought to the shores of this great country. How many generations of the world's poor and worthless was our gutless government going to let pollute the American continent? The Klans shall unite, state by state, run their own presidential slate next election, stem the tide.

Let this night be the spark that relights the fires of freedom. Amen.

And when our work is finished tonight, a little celebration. Down in Darktown. Help lighten the skin color of the next generation. Could be a real night to remember.

I checked my wristwatch. The klavern would be gathering soon. I was here early to scout any problems. Brought a helper.

James Scott was a big man, fearless, but slow in thought. I fetched him along—and his trench sweeper shotgun, of course—to help me get Nick DeCosta out of his cell. If

I could deliver him to the men of the klavern without their help, so much the better for my chances at rising to wizard.

I began to regret my decision the instant James laid eyes on that crow. It was about to peck out the eyes of Marshal Lawe's police dog, a big mean hound Lawe has the audacity to call Chief, making jest of our town's small peace-keeping force.

James didn't say a word, just picked up a rock and chunked it at the crow, hitting it squarely. Crow squawked loud enough to raise Lazarus, flew off like it was drunk. Chief started awake and barked his fool head off.

"We were trying to get to the cell quietly, James. Quietly."

He looked shamefaced and said, "I couldn't let that black carrion-eater hurt a fine dog, Jedediah. That ain't right."

The words were still in his mouth when the dog rushed at us.

"He doesn't appear grateful," I said.

Chief launched his considerable bulk through the air, catching James in the brisket and riding him to the ground. He took a nip of James' ear, then clamped his teeth in the Celt's shoulder. I have to admire that James heeded my admonition to be quiet, and struggled with the beast in silence.

For his part, Chief had too much muscle clamped between his teeth to do more than growl. They rolled at my feet, James trying to free himself, the dog determined to do his duty and guard the jail.

I cast about, found a length of firewood at the building's corner. I took a hefty swing, caught the back of Chief's skull, and laid the dog unconscious.

I watched James get to his feet, grimace as he tried to staunch the blood flowing from his shoulder. He turned to the dog and kicked it soundly in the side. I heard a rib snap, put my hand on his arm. He looked at me, a wild flame in his eyes.

"Business first," I said. "Klan business. Besides, I thought you didn't want to see such a fine canine hurt."

He said nothing, plucked his shotgun from the ground, and slammed his body against the jailhouse door.

It is begun. The Lord's will be done.

To both our surprise, the door was locked and bolted. James wasn't sure which shoulder to attend to, the one bleeding, or the one just bruised. He stood back, a puzzled expression on his face, and looked to me for instructions. I walked up and put my ear against the door.

"I don't hear a thing," I said. "Maybe the marshal has gone to dinner and just left the prisoner locked up."

"P'raps we can peek through the window and see what's what."

The front blinds were drawn, but light leaked out the edges. James put his eye to the crack for a moment. "I don't see anybody behind the counter."

I signaled him to follow and we went around back. I had him make a step with his clasped hands. I hoisted myself up and peered through the barred cell window. Let myself down.

"Nobody home," I said. "Maybe he moved the prisoner to the next town."

James shook his head. "I don't think so. My sister-in-law said she saw Lawe drive away about three quarters of an hour ago. Some good-looking woman was in the car with him, and a young man in the back seat."

I chewed on that for a minute. Thought to myself that

if DeCosta was gone and I hadn't done anything about it, it was going to look bad to the boys. I put my hand out for James' shotgun.

"Come on."

Marched back to the front entrance, brought the shotgun up, and blasted the lock completely off. Kicked twice, then the bolt gave way, and the door swung open. James was going to walk right in, but I held up my arm in warning. Sure enough, Constable Stubb rose up from behind the counter, pistol drawn. Looked ridiculous, a scrawny man in his late sixties trying to hold a big Colt .45 steady. Sweat on his forehead, and a tremble in his voice.

"You don't want to be doing this, Jedediah," Stubb said. "You'll be in a heap of trouble."

"That's my problem, not yours, and it's a problem for later. Right now I want to know where Nick DeCosta is."

"I'm a sworn officer of the law. I'm not going to give him up."

"Technically, I guess that would be true. You wouldn't be giving him up if you were dead."

James snapped his head toward me at that, not sure he wanted any part of killing a lawman.

"You can see what your choices are," I said. "Myself, I find it easy to judge both the quick and the dead." I cocked the hammer of the shotgun. Stared Stubbs in the eye, squeezed the trigger.

The gun bucked and roared and took out part of the counter two feet to the left of Stubbs. There was a commotion from behind the counter, down low, and out popped Nick on all fours, heading down the hall for the next room. I swatted the constable out of the way, noting that he'd wet himself, and took off after Nick.

James was close behind, and we fetched up against a stout door just as Nick locked it from inside. I jacked another round into the chamber and let fly.

The door lock shattered, and there was a yowl from inside the room. James went in and pulled out DeCosta, who was bleeding from a couple of pellet wounds.

"Those pellets smart, even though they're small, don't they?" I said.

Nick looked at me, pure hatred. Spat in my face and muttered something in a foreign tongue.

"You'll smart a deal more than that before the night's over."

VI. Chief

PAIN-PAIN, CHIEF HEAD hurt. Open eyes, dark, Chief blind? No, night come. See black things, swim in air. Black things kaws? No, close eyes, what happen?

Chief remember, hear "Kaaaw!" Wake up, Kaw fly away. See men, smell hate, bad men. Chief decide kill them, heh heh, kill them now.

Remember. Run, jump, snap ear, bite shoulder, feel good, taste man fear, taste blood. Chief good guard dog, hurt bad man, smell man hate, smell man fear. Chief feel battle joy, Chief happy.

Then world black, no sound, no smell. Not sleep.

Chief feel pain, much pain. Why? Chief bad dog? No, Chief not bad dog, Master say Chief good dog. Chief growl.

Chief feel tired, Chief sleep again? No.

Chief hear men come, man-barks, howls. What? Chief open eyes, see better.

Fog, night, men carry fire. Men run, not see Chief, men excited. Men show angry teeth, men yell. Chief smell hate. What, hate what?

Man-bitches come, bark, carry food baskets. Man-bitches excited, follow fire, show happy teeth.

Fire and fog, two-legs run, excited. Man-barks, howls, fear, hate, anger. And battle joy, yes, battle joy.

The Great Hunt! Great Hunt pass Chief!

Chief must run, must bark, Chief must kill, kill tonight. Chief want battle joy, yes.

Man-pups run, yip, show happy teeth, tiny teeth. Man-pups laugh.

Chief smell two-legs, smell fire. Little Bear here? No, Chief only dream Little Bear.

Chief run, Chief howl, Chief snap night sky, bite fog. Chief excited, Chief in Great Hunt, chase deer to sky. Chief live forever, Chief be Pack Leader.

Chief pass man-pups. Man-pups jump, show fear faces. Man-pup point, scream, "Wolf!" All man-pups scream, point.

Chief look behind. No wolf here, no wolfs in town, Chief never see wolf. Why man-pups scream wolf?

Chief lick mouth, taste blood, remember battle joy, show kill teeth. Man-pups scream, run.

Chief howl like wolf, bay at sky. Chief Pack Leader now.

Chief run fast-fast. Chief bark, bark loud. Man-bitches scatter. Man-bitch fall, drop food basket, food on ground. Chief hungry, Chief stop, eat. Food good, food belong Chief. Chief guard food, head down, growl, eat-eat.

Man-bitch scream, throw rock, rock hit Chief.

Chief look at man-bitch. Man-bitch show fear face, walk back fast-fast, man-bitch disappear in fog. Chief hear man-bitch scream, smell man-bitch fear. Why fear? Bitches serve Pack Leader, serve, not fear. Fear Pack Leader wrong.

No, Chief, no. Dog bitches serve Pack Leader, man-bitches serve men. One, two man-bitches fear men. Chief not man, Chief Pack Leader.

Chief serve Master? Yes. Pack Leader serve Master? Yes? No?

Where Master? Why gone?

Food gone, Chief head hurt, Chief thirsty. Chief go stream, find water, Chief drink-drink.

Chief hear Kaw, far in forest, Kaw calls. Chief hate Kaw.

Chief remember bad man, bad man have hate smell on him. Hate what?

Chief smell coon. Chief dream Little Bear hate coon, kill coon, eat coon. Chief hate coon, kill coon, Chief eat coon.

Chief smell smoke, hear men yell in forest, Chief run-run. Forest animals afraid, forest animals hide. Chief bay to Great Dog in Sky, Chief come, come now.

Chief smell fire, smoke hurt Chief eyes, Chief eyes make water. Much smoke, Chief smell only smoke, smoke hurt Chief nose.

Chief run, run fast, Chief side hurt. Why? Head hurt, eyes hurt, nose hurt, side hurt. Why?

Chief hear man scream, scream long time far away. What happen? Chief hear men bark, man-bitches yell, excited. Chief run fast-fast.

Clearing forest, big fire, many men, many man-bitches, many man-pups. Men in white outer skins, men yowl, men talk excited, men bark, man-bitches talk excited, bark, pull food from baskets. Man-pups laugh, man-pups cry, man-pups show fear face, man-pups talk excited, man-pups yowl, man-pups play, man-pups hide behind man-bitches.

New men come, men with guns, sticks. They fight with men in white outer skins. Blood on skin. Blood on ground. Chief smell battle–fear. Chief smell battle-joy.

Yes, battle-joy! Chief bark, Chief jump, bite. The battle-joy is here!

Hear scream from tree.

All look up in tree.

Chief smell meat burning. Did Master catch coon? Did Master burn coon for Little Bear? Little Bear eat coon? Coon in tree? No, no. Little Bear in Chief dream, not real.

Chief push man-pups, Chief bark. Man-pups scatter.

Chief push man-bitches, Chief bay. Man-bitches walk back fast.

Chief push men, show angry teeth, men walk back.

Chief see coon in tree, men burn coon. Little Bear must eat, eat now. Chief jump, bite meat, tear. Chief feel battle-joy, Chief eat. Little Bear eat!

Chief swallow.

No! Man-meat, Chief eat man-meat. Wrong! Chief bad dog. Chief not Pack Leader, Chief bad dog.

Chief run away.

Chief hide, Chief ashamed.

Chief want die.

VII. Kaw

THE ROCK HURT me and I flew into a tree-with-thick-leaves, hiding myself in the shadow. Why did bad man stop me from pecking the Barker's eyes? It was not his business, business.

Why did Bright-Eye make men? The world would be a better place without them, without them.

At dusk I tried to fly. It hurt, but I could move. I found a family of Squeakers in a cornfield and ate them all. My stomach was full, but still I felt the pain of the rock against my body, my body.

Bright-Eye went behind the mountains. Mist came up from the creek, slowly like a Meower, moving from tree to tree. I wish Kaws could move like that, like that.

But Meowers cannot fly, and flying is better, flying is best. Kaws fly up into sky with Bright-Eye, feel wind in feathers, see everything, like Bright-Eye does.

And at night, Bright-Eye is gone behind the mountains, but Kaws can still fly the sky, watch the ground, find the food. Kaws are best animals of all. Kaws are smart. I am a Kaw. I am smart, smart.

I am smarter than Bright-Eye. I would not make men. I would not make Barkers. I would not make Meowers. Only trees and Kaws and Squeakers. Bright-Eye would stay in sky all the time, not hide behind mountains, mountains.

Maybe someday I will take Bright-Eye's place, run the world better. Yes, a Kaw would be a better god. I will be a better god, better god.

I preened. I put my head beneath my wing to sleep.

THE NOISE WOKE me. Men, many of them. They carried branches that were on fire. Then came women, with children. With food. I flew into the night sky to watch from above, but the mist made it hard to see. The crowd went into the forest, the forest.

I flew from tree to tree. Man food is good. When I am Bright-Eye I will let there be a few women to make man-food, man-food.

I followed the food. Deep into the forest. Too much noise. Too many people. The forest animals were afraid. They ran away or hid. Only a brave Kaw like me stayed to see what the men would do.

And then something happened to make even me afraid, afraid.

The men put on new heads. Tall and white and pointed heads, pointed heads.

One man-with-a-new-head shouted at the others. They brought one man forward. He did not have a new head. There was blood on his face, blood on his feathers, feathers.

Two men-with-new-heads tied this one with a vine. They tied his hands. They tied his neck. They threw the vine into a tree, a tree.

Women and children gathered branches and twigs and made a pile around the man-with-blood.

One man-with-a-new-head threw his burning branch into the pile and it made fire. The man-with-blood-on-his-face shouted, then screamed, screamed.

They pulled the vine in the tree and the man was lifted into the air over the fire. He screamed and screamed. His legs tried to run in the air, but he did not run away. He could not fly away because he was only a stupid man with no wings, no wings.

His feathers began to smoke, to smoke.

Kaws do not like smoke. It is hard to fly in smoke. A Kaw cannot see, a Kaw cannot breathe. I will not let there be fire when I am Bright-Eye, Bright-Eye.

I put my head beneath my wing. The smoke was not so bad that way. I listened to the screams. And then laughs, and the yells, and shouts.

And always the screams, the screams.

I heard the Barker come. He barked, he bayed, he snarled. He jumped onto the smoking body of man-with-blood and bit off a piece. I saw him swallow it. And then the Barker ran away into the forest and made no more sounds, no more.

I STAYED WAITING for the Light-Before-Bright-Eye-Comes. The children were gone. The women were gone. The men-with-new-heads were gone. The food was gone. The fire was gone. Now only a little smoke, little smoke.

The man-with-blood had stopped screaming long ago, long ago.

I flew into the clearing, looking around. Nothing. No movement. No animals.

I landed on the head of man-with-blood. He did not move. His eyes were open, but they did not see, not see.

I pecked them out, those eyes, one by one. I felt great pride. I felt like a god. I shouted "Kaaaaaaaaaaaaaw!"

I am as powerful as Bright-Eye. I took the eyes-of-a-man, eyes-of-a-man.

And when I see the stupid Barker I will take his, too.

Yes! The Barker's eyes, too.

VIII. Kleagle

"TIME TO DON your hoods," I told them. I pulled on my own, adjusting the scarlet insignia of Kleagle correctly.

"Let me put mine on after I tie him up, Jedediah," said James. "It's hard to see through those little eyeholes."

I looked at him coldly. "When I wear the hood, you are to address me as Kleagle, not by my Christian name." I motioned to two men who already had their hoods on. "You two truss up this sorry piece of trash."

By the light of the torches the evening took on the appearance of a summer's night church picnic. The children played, chased one another, while the women set out the picnic baskets.

The preacher, from beneath his hood, blessed the meal and all those who would partake of it. After the meal—for dessert, as it were—the klavern secretary read the list of charges against the foreigner. The klansmen deliberated in an orderly manner, finally settling on execution by hanging with fire.

I set the women and children to the task of building the pyre. They made a game of it, a contest to see who could gather the most tinder.

"Hoist him up by the limb of that tree."

James tried to get back in my graces by volunteering

to set things ablaze. I let him. Some folks are squeamish about such things.

The Italian began to roar. I motioned to the sergeant at arms. He struck the wop twice in the face, silencing him for a bit.

The men pulled on the rope, which dragged him through the fire, and then left him dangling over it.

DeCosta screamed like a woman. It went on and on. When he wasn't screaming he was begging for his life. I don't know when I've seen such a degrading spectacle.

His shoes began to smoke and he used one to prize off the other. Then he began to kick his feet, like he was trying to high step around some hot pavement.

"Lookit that," said some wag. "I believe he's got the jake-leg."

"Naw. He's jitterbugging, that's what he's doing."

There was general laughter, then women and children began to scream. I heard a large hound barking and baying.

And at the same time, state militia came marching from the tree line and began to swing their truncheons.

How did they get here?

Even if the constable had phoned after he came to, it was more than three hours by truck from the nearest base. That meant someone had betrayed our whereabouts even earlier.

The womenfolk tried to get the children out of harm's way, running for the woods around the clearing. The militia let them escape, then set about the klavern with ferocity. I figured most of them were Boston Irish, so it was Knights of Columbus against the Knights of the Invisible Empire.

The men in our klavern are mostly veterans, well

used to the ways of war. They gave as good as they got, but there were too many militia for this to turn out any way but bad.

I decided it was time to fade into the trees. As I left I saw something that seemed like a vision from Hades.

Marshal Lawe's dog Chief burst into the inner circle around the condemned man, snarling and gnashing his teeth like he had the hydrophobia. He took one look at the body dangling in midair and made a tremendous leap. He bit a chunk of flesh from DeCosta, then stood glaring at us, his eyes glowing as if possessed.

No sooner had the creature swallowed down the grisly morsel than he seemed to shrink in on himself, the light dying out of his eyes. He put his tail between his legs, slunk off into the woods. I saw nothing further of the hound.

I WENT BACK to the clearing a little after midnight. The militia were gone, though they had cordoned off the area with a rope and some warning flags. Nothing much left but a few trampled picnic baskets.

And of course Nick hanging there. I figured the state police would return at sunup to investigate.

Meanwhile I'd stand watch, make sure no leftover sparks set the woods on fire.

You have to do your duty as a citizen.

LAWE REDUX

Live free or die;
Death is not the worst of evils.
— *General John Stark, New Hampshire*

Yeah, but it's no picnic, neither.
— *Marshal Lawe*

I.

WHEN I GOT to the jail in the morning, I set the county maintenance man to fixing the door that had been busted. I looked at the door and the blast pattern, figured it to be a shotgun had done it.

The mist from the night before had lifted and it looked to be a hot day. Without any rain in the last week the dust was liable to rise at the slightest breeze. I looked about for Chief but he wasn't to be found.

That was mighty unusual. Chief always had his nose in my hand first thing in the morning, hoping I had a treat for him.

Constable Stubb was still on duty, looking older than his years for having been awake all night. He took me through the events of the night before, and I didn't let on that I had listened in on the police car radio.

The way he told it this morning, he was more heroic than he had sounded last night, but I let it go. We all like to spruce up our history a bit. By the time I'm eighty I'm sure I'll have been a wonder when I was thirty. But then he added something interesting.

"It was 'bout one in the ayem when Granny MacKay showed up with a couple of her nephews, big boys. I was sure there was gonna be more trouble," said Stubb.

"They try to break out Angus and Andrew?"

"Jist the opposite. She told them boys to stay put.

Brought 'em some clean clothes and warmer blankets, a nice picnic basket for breakfast. Said she didn't want there to be no question of their whereabouts last night, not with the lynching of Nick DeCosta and all."

"So she already knew that DeCosta had been strung up?"

"Sure did. And the militia hadn't been broadcasting that about."

"Still, I suppose anyone who had been there when it happened could have told her," I said.

"Maybe. But most folks was in custody or still hiding out in the woods."

"So what's your thought on this, Stubb?"

"I think she knowed about it ahead of time."

"Can't prove it from what you've told me so far."

"Just giving you my thoughts, Marshal."

II.

I waive the quantum of the sin
The hazard of concealing:
But, och! it hardens a' within,
And petrifies the feeling!
Epistle to a Young Friend
— *Robert Burns*

I TOOK THE forest service road as far as I could, then set out on foot the rest of the way to the meadow where Nick had been killed. In the shade of the trees it was still cool.

As the sun heated the tops of the trees I caught the scent of pine sap rising. It was pitcher-perfect lovely there. I heard a black-cap titmouse drawling its melancholy "te-derry" deeper in the woods. The early morning gnats had settled so my walk was cumftable enough, as walks to the scene of a murder go.

When I got to the clearing I expected to see a great deal of industry. The militia had been out since sunrise and it was near eight now. I thought there'd be a military operation in full swing to find the murderers.

Instead what I saw was about twenty men standing guard on a perimeter, rifles slung over their shoulders, looking as bored as only soldiers on pointless duty can look. Another thirty militiamen lounged in the shade at the edge of the clearing.

I sought out the commanding officer, a second louie named Able, and introduced myself. I asked why nothing was happening.

"We were told to wait for the county prosecutor, a Mr. Sykes."

"Big Bill Sykes is coming out here?" I said. "What in tarnation does a lawyer expect to do, serve the corpse a search warrant?"

"You know more'n I do. I just wait for orders."

"How long you boys been here?"

"You mean this morning? Or last night?"

"Why don't you give me the sequence of events?" I had been waiting to use that line ever since I read it in one of those stories in *Police Gazette*.

Able went through it a couple of times but I couldn't make sense of it. The militia base was two and a half, maybe three hours drive from Peony Springs, yet they had arrived in town at 9:30. By the time they found the "riot" they had been called to break up it was 10 pm. And yet Stubb had told me that Jedediah Spout and James Scott had taken Nick from the jail at 8:30.

Stubbs was right. No one in town could have called it in soon enough for the militia to arrive when they did. Someone had tipped off the state troopers ahead of time, certainly before things turned deadly.

That led me to wonder who that someone was. The only person that made sense to me was Judge Halbertson. He might have feared that vigilante justice would make him look bad come next election.

Doc Lowe, who doubled as the county coroner, arrived

carrying his black bag, puffing at the unaccustomed walk. He supervised the cutting down of the corpse, and took his time before he declared the person to be dead, which made the militamen snicker. He began a preliminary examination of the corpse.

"Anybody able to identify the deceased?" said Doc.

With reluctance I walked over and did my best. I hated seeing that charred face with the tongue sticking out that-away. And the eyes was missing. The face was blackened so much I wasn't a hundred percent certain it was Nick. But I saw that he had on the same clothes as yesterday afternoon, so I signed off for the identification.

"How come he's missing the one shoe?" said Lieutenant Able.

Doc just shrugged and continued his examination of the body. I walked away a few feet and began to examine the scene in an organized fashion, making notes in a little book I brung along for the purpose.

One of the militiamen called to me. "You might want to see this."

I went and picked up a brass shell casing. I sniffed it and could smell that it had been fired recently. It warn't a leftover from last spring's deer season. It was thirty caliber, could have been fired by any of the Springfield rifles in town. I believe half the male population owns one of them war surplus weapons.

I showed it to Doc and he tried to find a bullet wound, but to no effect.

"Coulda been somebody just firing into the air in the excitement," said Able.

"Yeah, coulda." I made a note.

III.

If once a man indulges himself in murder, very soon he comes to think little of robbing; and from robbing he comes next to drinking and Sabbath-breaking, and from that to incivility and procrastination.

> *Murder Considered as One of the Fine Arts*
> — *Thomas De Quincy*

NEAR HALF AN hour later Big Bill Sykes came blustering into the clearing. He was dressed to kill, I tell you. Silk tie, hat, pin-stripe suit. But he didn't look happy about how dusty his spats was. Trailing him was a news photographer and that woman journalist I had seen in the courtroom. She wasn't from our local paper, but some big city rag.

Big Bill told everyone within earshot that he was in charge now, this was going to be a county special investigation. None of the militiamen nor I was specially impressed, but the reporter was all agog. Meantime the photographer looked like he'd been to a dozen lynchings already that day and one more weren't worth mussing his hair.

Sykes launched into a spiel about how the Klan was a Scourge Upon This State and Someone Needed To Do

Something. He was practically talking in headlines and I figger it was well rehearsed. Little miss reporter took it all down in shorthand.

About then it clicked for me who had called in the militia.

"The state should have done something back in 1924 when the Klan rioted in Worcester," said Sykes. "If we'd acted then, we wouldn't be having these problems still. I fear it's time for someone with real backbone to take the helm and guide the ship of state away from the shoals of bigotry and prejudice."

One of the militiamen began to laugh as he listened to this hogwash, but he turned it into a coughing fit when his commander caught his eye.

"I think you should have brung your soapbox, Big Bill," I said. "Though it wouldn't have done any good. None of these boys vote in this county."

The reporter tore her gaze away from Big Bill, and looked at me with shining eyes. "They'll be able to vote for him when he runs for the state's senate seat in the fall."

"I didn't know he was running," I said dryly.

"I haven't even thought of running," said Big Bill, and that lie came out so smooth I knew he had a good chance of winning.

The reporter said, "You'll think about it when you see our next editorial."

Now it was time for Big Bill to pretend he was a detective. He ordered the militiamen to form a line at arm's width apart, then march across the meadow, looking for clues.

Turned out to be an interesting technique. Since the meadow was full of picnic trash from the Klansmen who'd been there last night, everybody had the thrill of finding a piece of "evidence." Big Bill would hustle over, looking intelligent, trailed by the reporter and photographer. After the first ten pieces of debris, the enthusiasm of the press waned. Big Bill kept responding to calls for his help, but started looking glum.

I, however, was entertained as all get out.

About twenty minutes into the exercise a man hollered that he'd found something, but in a voice that said maybe he really had. Even I went over to see what was up.

It was the dangdest turn of events I've come across.

Who had shot a crow? And why? And why last night, right here?

Doc come over to take a look. He pulled at the birds wings.

"The rigor indicates it died about nine, ten hours ago."

He held the bird's body so the light shown into the gaping wound the bullet had made. His face got a funny look.

"I can see the stomach contents." he said, and turned it so I could see.

"I guess we know what happened to Nick DeCosta's eyes now."

The militiaman who had found the crow turned aside and tossed his breakfast into the dry grass.

One of the militiamen who wasn't on "evidence" duty came up and tapped my arm.

"Marshal, I'm a mountain boy, done lots of tracking in country just like this," he said.

"I'm listening."

"I believe we ought to check out a trace over on the far side of the meadow."

I told Big Bill he was still in charge of evidence collection. Doc detailed four of the militia to get Nick's body onto a blanket and to carry it out to a pickup truck to take back to the county morgue. I asked Lieutenant Able to release the tracker to me, and the two of us started off.

IV.

Revenge converts a little right
into a great wrong.
— *German Proverb*

I'D NEVER BEEN much of a hunter, but once Mike—that
was the militiaman's name—showed me what to look
for, things came pretty clear. Something heavy had been
dragged out of the meadow by two people, one of 'em
much bigger than the other. Mike thought it was probably
a man and a woman, though it could have been a boy.

We followed the trail for a couple of hundred yards,
lost the track at the rocky edge of a ravine. The day's heat
was upon us and our passage stirred up flies and
midges.

I was feeling pure misery, what with the sun and the
bugs. We stood at the edge while Mike scanned along the
stones looking for further trace.

I was ready to go back and said so. Mike held up his
hand for silence, so I shet up and listened hard.

I heard it now. A droning coming from the bottom
of the ravine. Sounded like a million insects was busy
down there.

We picked our way down the rocky slope, with Mike
commenting now and then when he saw some scuff mark
or bit of different colored dirt. At the bottom was a sight

I don't care to see again in this life or the next.

A body was lying there, half covered in mould and duff. Flies was buzzing around it fierce.

We went closer. I didn't need Doc to tell me this was fresh. Looked like the body had been completely buried, then someone had dug it partway up. The why of that was obvious in one way, but difficult to understand in another.

Whoever had dug it up had done great violence to the face of the corpse. It was mangled and had gaping wounds, with strips of flesh hanging offen it. It was unrecognizable and seemed to indicate an attack of great fury. There was no blood, so the man had been already dead.

But why attack a dead man? And who was he?

Mike and I searched through the pockets and found a billfold, with a driver's license inside.

Jedediah Spout.

Now what the hell?

Jackie Sue Unleashed

But wild Ambition loves to slide, not stand,
And Fortune's ice prefers to Virtue's land.
— *John Dryden*

I.

I'D BEEN PETTING the possum and finally drifted off to sleep about midnight, having warmish dreams of the sea. Couldn't have been more than half an hour before a ruckus woke me up. I heard Ma and Daddy talking downstairs so I crept out of my room and looked through the banister.

Daddy was a sight. Blood was running down his face and his shirt was soaked pretty good. He staggered when he moved and Ma began a low howl I'd never heard before, sort of sounded like the wind blowing and moaning through the eves.

I wanted to go down and see what had happened, but something told me I better stay put. Adults don't cotton to their children—no matter how mature, I'm sure—anyway, they don't cotton to their children knowing all their secrets.

"I knew no good would come of this, Eugene," said my Ma.

"Let's leave the 'I told you so' until later," said Daddy "If ever."

Ma pushed him down into a chair and began moving her fingers through his hair, a sight more gently than she ever did mine when she was untangling knots. She clucked at what she saw, then went into the kitchen and brought back a towel and a bowl of water. She cleaned the blood from his forehead, working her way toward the source.

"This is going to need stitches. And that means Doc Lowe's going to know you were there, plus whatever nurse is working for him."

Daddy looked grieved. "Can't you do it yourself? You sewed up those tears in the milk cow's teat when she tried to jump the bob wire."

"I can't put a needle through your scalp. It'll give you too much pain."

"So I have to do it myself? Bile me some thread and a needle, Martha."

Ma wrung her hands. Until that moment I had always thought that was just an expression old folks used.

"Hurry up, woman. It's not going to stop bleeding by magic."

"Hush up. I'll do it."

She brought a teapot of boiling water from the kitchen, and got the dry goods from the breakfront in the dining room. While she poured the water over the thread and needle, Daddy got out some of Granny MacKay's best stuff, put the jug on his shoulder, and took a swig straight from the neck. Ma looked peeved when he did it, but said nothing.

She put in the stitches and it made me smart just to watch. Daddy eyes teared up and to cover it he talked about the militia using their billies pretty freely and wondered aloud who had ratted on the Knights.

That got my attention. Any time those boys were involved bad things just seemed to happen. Ma and Daddy lowered their voices a bit and seemed to be skirting around something. I lay flat against the carpet so I could hear better, getting a nose full of must and something that smelled suspiciously like mouse.

"I don't know what's going to come of her," said Daddy. "I could see some of the women casting a look at me, like I was part to blame, even as they strung him up."

Ohmigawd, they hung Angus. I put a fist in my mouth to stifle a gasp.

"They should have put the son with the father and hanged them both," said Ma.

Oh. Not Angus, just Nick.

That didn't make much sense to me, but little about the kluxers does. At least this wouldn't keep me from my plans. I thought about Hollywood some and missed part of what Ma said next. But I heard this:

"It's her fault as much as his, maybe more. The way she swings her tits around, puts her elbows back, it's like to drive the boys crazy. And she knows it."

"I'm afraid she's going to wind up with child," said Daddy, looking ominous. "Or worse. Shame us all." He took another swig and squinted at Ma. "I think this comes from your side of the family. And you haven't done much to set her on the righteous path."

"Oh, I haven't?" said Ma, looking dangerous. "Fathers don't have any part in raising daughters?"

"You know I can't talk to her about female things. That wouldn't be right." He took one last drink from the jug and put the stopper back. "I'm thinking maybe she needs to live with my Aunt Dolene in North Dakota. Not much trouble she can get into out there on the high plains."

"Well, I don't know, Eugene," said Ma, in that kind of whiny way she has when she's gonna give in but thinks she needs to make a point first.

I'd heard enough. More than enough. It was time to go.

I crept into my parents' room quiet as I could be and pulled open Ma's bottom dresser drawer. I knew that's where she kept her pin money and I figured I was entitled to half if she was willing to ship me to the North Pole like that.

Turned out she only had seven dollars. I didn't know things were so tight, so I only took five, since I'd been expecting there to be twenty bucks or so. My conscience gave me a little pinch, but I just pinched it right back. What had it done for me lately?

I saw a brand new pair of silk step-ins. They must have been a gift from Daddy, for they still had the ribbon on them.

Shoot, they were already married. What did they need those for? They couldn't still be doing it at their ages. I took the step-ins, too. I pulled out the family suitcase from beneath my folks' bed to pack them in. Then I grabbed a shirt of my dad's, a pair of his old pants, and a flat brimmed driver's cap he liked to use when he drove the wagon.

On the way back to my room, I opened the door to my brothers' room and stared at them for a long moment, wondering if I should shed a tear or not. I don't have anything against the two brats, not really. They just ain't too bright. Actually they're perfect for life in this little hole of a town. I blew 'em a kiss and closed the door.

Back in my room I packed my best clothes. I pulled back the curtain and let the moonlight in. I sat in front of my mirror in that silvery light and cut my hair into as short a bob as I could. No more cutesy girl curls. I was a woman from this moment forth.

Well, maybe after the next day. For the time being I altered my dad's shirt and pants to fit me and dressed as a boy. I had to wind some flannel about my bosom to flatten it.

I realized that with a flat chest and short hair I looked like a flapper. I liked that.

I heard my folks coming up the stairs and I slid between the covers of my bed, feigning sleep, but peering out from beneath my lashes. Wouldn't you know but Ma and Daddy cracked open my door and looked in on me all sorrowful. I guess the decision had been made.

Ma hadn't even argued that long.

II.

Low Ambition and the thirst of praise.
— *William Cowper*

I WAITED TWO hours until I was sure they were asleep and then I snuck barefoot downstairs and out the back door. I sat and put on my socks, but realized the only shoes I had that fit me were girl shoes. They'd give me away in a second.

It was a mile walk, but I got to the Thornton place near four a.m. and swiped a pair of Johnny's shoes from where I knew he left them on the porch at night, his ma not wanting him to track farm muck into her kitchen. He was a year older than me, but about my size, and his shoes fit fine.

I thought about leaving my shoes in place of his as a joke, kind of like the brownies had swapped shoes between two farms. Good sense took hold and I decided that was too big a clue as to my trail, so I tossed my shoes into their well and set off down the road toward town at a brisk pace.

Oh my, but the freedom I felt! Walking in the chill air, seeing the false dawn, listening to the night peepers. I chucked a rock at a sleeping cow and watched it twitch awake and look about all fearful. Made me laugh, I'll say.

What a blessing it is to be alive!

After another twenty minutes I was thinking what a blessing it would have been if I'd thought to grab some food from either my house or the Thornton's. It was getting pretty light now and I'd hit the main road. I made a right at the next turning so I could skirt town. No sense tempting fate and have some early riser busybody see me walking down Main Street.

I hitched a ride with a delivery van that was going to the next county. The driver seemed to be a little slow in the head, but not an actual idiot or anything. I helped the guy unload several crates of produce by way of thanks and got off in Angus DeCosta's hometown.

I pocketed two apples and an orange as a tip. Also the pack of cigarettes he left on the dashboard.

It was after seven and I found a café open. I fished out some change from my pants pocket, which felt both mighty funny while being convenient at the same time. It was like having a pocketbook built into your clothes, you know? Anyway, a cup of joe and two doughnuts later I felt like a new woman.

Or man, depending on how you looked at me. And the guy behind the counter had been eyeballing me kind of funny, but he didn't say anything.

By now people were beginning to be out and about. I asked around for the DeCosta place. A nice old lady, probably forty or so, pointed me in the right direction and said:

"Wasn't that a shame?"

"A shame?"

"Didn't you hear? They hanged Nick DeCosta over in Potemkin County last night. The Klan was behind it from what I hear."

"The Klan?" I said. "Not in Potemkin County."

"You didn't hear it from me, but they're like lice. They're everywhere, you cain't get rid of them, and they're no end of irritation."

"What's going to come of it?" I asked.

"I heard tell the state militia is putting the town under martial law until order is restored and they find the culprits."

I thanked her for her time and followed her directions to Angus' house.

That turned out to be a stinker.

I knew the signs. All the shades were drawn. There was black crepe over the front door. Nothing stirred.

The DeCostas were in mourning and no one but family was welcome to ring that bell or knock at that door until there'd been a funeral or wake. Course I heard they're of the Catholic persuasion so they may have some pagan practice I'm not familiar with.

But still it looked as if I was going to have to bide my time until I put my plan into action. I decided to nose around their backyard and see if there was someplace I could hole up. Maybe I could catch Angus if he came outside for a chore or something.

EBENEEZER REVISITED

The heart of man is the place the devils dwell in:
I feel sometimes a hell within myself.
Religio Medici
— *Sir Thomas Browne*

I.

AS I SAY, my eyes at night ain't what they used to be. I was walking back by myself to find Lars, but the moon kept ducking behind the clouds. When it did I had to stand stock still for a few moments, hoping for my eyes to adjust. Or better yet for the moon to come back out. I wisht Darnell was there to be my eyes.

Whenever the moon broke through the clouds I hurried as best I could without tripping. I wanted to put that fateful scene behind me.

I was probably a hundred yards from the remains of our campfire. Lars must never have awakened and the fire was dying out. When the moon disappeared again, I tried to navigate using the embers' red glow, but I stubbed my foot against a rock and came down sudden-like.

I sat on my butt in some deep duff nursing my knee, which had twisted as I went down. I heard something moving nearby and I froze. Whatever it was, it was of a good size, not a squirrel or skunk. Not big enough to be a bear, though. Plus I didn't think there were any left this close to town. Smaller than a wild cat, too.

What was peculiar was the dragging sound, followed by a soft double thump. I have to say my arms was covered in gooseflesh.

The moonlight returned but I blinked more than

once at what that cold light revealed. It was the largest possum I had ever seen, maybe thirty-five, forty pounds. Its back legs appeared to be broken or paralyzed and they dragged behind as the possum pulled itself along by its front paws.

If that weren't peculiar enough there were four possums of normal size walking alongside the big one, sort of like attendants on a queen.

I had been holding my breath for some time and at last had to exhale. When I did the nearest possum snapped its head around. It came right over to me, looked me up and down. It opened its mouth wide, and moonlight glinted off them toothy needles. When it was satisfied I was not a threat, it turned its back on me and resumed its escort duty.

I was shaken. I had never before seen such a thing and I wished I hadn't seen it now. I was too old for surprises.

It was more than that, of course. It seemed to be a return to my boyhood, when I had gone walking with my grandfather in the forest. He had passed on the lore and folktales of the Cherokee. Those tales were full of chance meetings with animals, meetings that always foretold something of importance.

The difference now was that Grampa wasn't here to tell me what this meant. It just seemed mysterious and sinister to me.

Coulda been this was a sign of something coming, something bad. But what?

Or maybe it was a sign that the old queen was dying. But what old queen? And dying of broken legs? See, that's the problem with signs from the animals. They ain't all that clear.

I was left with an uneasy feeing as I made my way back to camp, and I had been jumpy to begin with. The woods seemed full of evil tonight and Darnell was out there armed with my rifle and anger in his heart.

When I reached the campsite I stirred up the fire with a stick and Lars with the toe of my boot. Over my eighty-one years I've found that most drunks don't wake up happy and Lars was no exception. There was a deal of grumbling and cursing, followed by coughing and spitting. I put a couple of sticks on the fire, then thought better of it and pulled them out again.

"You lost your mind, Eben? Leave that wood in there, let the fire build. It's cold already and gonna get colder."

"I need you to hesh up and listen, Lars. There's worse happening than we thought."

I told him what Darnell and I had seen. I didn't mention the queen possum, though. I was afraid he'd think I'd gone queer in the head. Besides, that hanging man was problem enough.

"Who was it they lynched?" said Lars.

"I ain't sure. Couldn't recognize him in the dark, plus his face was all black from the smoke. But I'd say it was a white man from the clothes he had on."

Lars thought about it. "Could be that DeCosta boy."

"Seemed too big to me, but maybe."

We both knew we ought to get out of there but we didn't know what we should do or where to go next.

"Darnell stayed behind with your rifle?"

I nodded.

"No good's gonna come of that. Why'd you let him have it?"

I didn't bother answering that.

"And he said that crow was a fetch?" said Lars. "I haven't heard that term since I was a child."

"He said it was meant to fetch the dead man's soul to hell."

"My pappy said a fetch was an escort to Niflheim."

"To where?"

"I come from Viking stock, at least that what my folks liked to believe. If you were a warrior who died fighting you went to Valhalla."

"Yeah, I heard of that place from a man in my platoon. Rest of us thought he was crazy. Kinda liked the battle stories he told, though. Least until he was blowed up in our first real fight. But he never talked about a Sniffle-wine."

"Niffle hime." Lars sounded it out. "It's where the women and kids and men who die of old age go. Guess it'd be kind of like hell to a Viking."

"I don't put much stock in such things," I said.

We were talking around our real problem and we knew it. I put together our pans and utensils, bundled them for travel. Lars wrapped himself in his blanket and began to kick dirt over the embers.

I motioned for him to stop.

"What is it?" said Lars.

I put my finger to my lips and pointed.

II.

Black spirits and white, red spirits and gray,
Mingle, mingle, mingle, you that mingle may.
The Witch
— *Thomas Middleton*

COMING THROUGH THE forest, maybe fifty yards away, was a woman in light colored clothes. I felt a cold pour over me like icy molasses. I looked at Lars and saw that his hair was rising up.

"Who's that?" said Lars.

"At the Battle of First Manassas there was a woman killed," I said. "Her ghost come back to the Second Battle of Manassas and walked the field. They called her the woman in white."

"Why you tellin' me that story?"

"I was at both those battles and I think that's her. Back to look for the dying."

Lars wrapped his blanket tighter and reached for the bottle of rye, but it had been emptied long ago.

The woman in white came up to us and stopped on the other side of the campfire embers, staring. The heat still rising from the coals made her apparition shimmer in the cold night air.

Her head was huge and out of shape, like maybe it had been hit by a musket butt. One eye was black and when the moonlight caught it, there was no white to it. It was like a black marble in the socket. The lips was puffy and split. Up close though, her dress wasn't anything from the 1860s, it was a modern housedress.

The apparition held its hands out toward the embers, warming them. The battered lips parted and it spoke. I couldn't make out what it said at first, but it repeated. Its speech was as mangled as its mouth.

"Why you fella' out heah?"

Lars was trembling. I could tell he wanted a drink in the worst way. He tried to speak but couldn't get any words out.

I figured if a ghost asks you a question it's only prudent to answer.

"We was just having a little hunting party."

The apparition's eyes glittered at that. She clenched her left hand, and that made me notice the wedding ring upon its third finger. The right hand went into the pocket of her dress and seemed to fondle something.

"I'm huntin', too. A man."

She pulled her hand from her pocket and showed us a tooth lying there in her palm.

Lars choked out, "Who?"

I think he was afraid it was himself the apparition was hunting. The next words froze us.

"Jedediah Spou'. Have you see' him?"

Lars started and gave out a low cry. He pointed back along the path I had come.

"He's over that way."

"You saw him?" said the ghost, leaning forward in eagerness.

Lars shook his head violently and she turned her eerie gaze on me.

"Bout half a mile, in a clearing," I said, my voice shaking. "But you don't want to go there. They's hanged a man."

"Tha's no' my business. I come to send Jedediah straigh' to hell. Jus' Jed."

And with that she walked out of the campsite and into the forest. The moon went behind the clouds for a few seconds and when it broke through again, she was gone.

"So you don't put much stock in such things?" said Lars. "If that ain't a fetch, I don't know what is."

I had to agree. I was shivering with a chill unrelated to the night's temperature. Something else was bothering me.

"What about Darnell?"

GRANNY REUNITED

This reasonable moderator,
and equal piece of justice,
Death.
> *Religio Medici*
> — *Sir Thomas Browne*

I.

MY NITWIT NEPHEW had stoppered the still too tight. About 10:15 the pressure built up and it exploded. The slobbercock shot across the yard and came through my window, a copper rocket that broke the mirror over my dresser and scared Pyewacket out of six of her lives.

I had my hair up in papers and my nightdress on, so I was of no mind to go outside and fix the damage. However, someone needed to douse the burner and see if any mash could be saved.

I pulled on heavy overalls, donned a navy watch cap, and put on my husband's old peacoat. It gave me a pang to catch his scent for a moment as I slipped into it, though he's been gone these five years now.

Memory. I am not sure if it's a blessing or a torment.

I had finished my task when two more of my nephews roared up in their battered truck. As they got out, I realized it wasn't only the truck that was battered.

I hustled them into the kitchen and got some coffee into them while cleaning their wounds. They told me what had happened.

I already knew about the Klan and Nick, for I had helped to plan it with Big Bill Sykes. I had not expected my own kin to be so dim as to involve themselves.

"What is wrong with you? You two have not gone and

joined the Klan, have you? That would make no sense at all, the KKK being such rabid Prohibitionists."

"Well, Granny, that's what the Klucks preach, all right, but a lot of them boys still like a gargle now and then. Some of our best customers, doncha know."

"And you say the state militia broke up the lynch mob? Did they come in from the armory or the capital?"

"The capital."

I thought that over. Someone must have called in an alert before things were actually under way for them to have showed up at the time they did. I knew about it, Sykes knew about it, the Kleagle knew about it for sure. But Marshal Lawe was no dummy either. Perhaps he had guessed there would be trouble.

Or, considering the brainpower of some of my kin, maybe someone mentioned it to him.

"Was Marshal Lawe with the militia?" I said.

"No, ma'am."

Perhaps he had stayed away to stave off repercussions from the MacKay family. It would be hard to point the finger at him if he had not been a part of the riot squad. I came to a decision.

"I want you boys to get two more drivers and trucks. With Nick DeCosta dead, all his belongings pass to Mary Elizabeth. And she is kin. You go pick up all the cases of Nick's goods—get the best stuff first if you need two trips—and get it into our own storage. She is likely to be easy prey for the other shiners in her county."

The boys shuffled their feet and finally Horace spoke.

"Don't you think there's going to be guards with guns over at the DeCosta warehouse?"

"Of course there will be. That is why I am leaving in five minutes to clear the path with Mary Elizabeth. By the time you get the crew together I will have made the arrangements."

II.

> As is the mother,
> So is her daughter.
> — *Ezekiel 16:44*

I WAS DRIVING the Buick Roadster and needed the pea-coat against the wind. It took more than half an hour to reach my daughter's home.

I had never been able to visit her there while Nick was alive, but I had driven by on more than one occasion, hoping for a glimpse of her or my grandson. It never happened.

Once I was within a block, I shut off the engine and coasted up to the house.

The lights were off inside and I wondered if she had heard the news. I sat for a few moments gathering my thoughts. This needed the right approach.

The porch light came on and the front door opened. Mary Elizabeth had a robe about her. She waved that I should come up to the door. Of a sudden I was nervous. We had not spoken in more than a dozen years.

When I got to the porch and she saw what I was wearing, she smiled briefly. She spoke in a low voice.

"I see you didn't dress up for the occasion, Mother."

"I thought it important I get here as quickly as possible. I was working outside when I got the—" I broke off, unsure of myself for the first time in many years. "I fear you might need some company tonight."

She gave me a searching look. "Why would that be?"

"Oh, Mary Elizabeth. I am afraid that I must tell you something dreadful."

"If you mean that my bastard husband is dead, I got a telephone call ten minutes ago. I pretty much figured you would be close behind."

"You already know?" Something was out of joint.

"I could see which way the wind was blowing, Mother. I was in Peony Springs today."

"I did not see you in court, Daughter."

"The marshal thought I mightn't be safe on the streets of my old hometown. Too many MacKays about. I was in seclusion."

"And yet you sensed there might be trouble?"

"That's why I got Angus back here before dark. I didn't want him caught up in it."

I had forgotten how intelligent my youngest child was. It made me wonder what else she already knew. A breeze came up and I shivered, against my will.

"May we talk inside?" I said. "It is quite cold on the porch."

"I don't want to wake Angus just yet. It's going to be a long day tomorrow, and he'll have just heard of his father's death. There will be funeral arrangements to make, crepe to hang, identification of the body. A full schedule."

She watched me for a long moment, her breath showing in the night air.

"I'll get us some coffee," she said. "We can sit in your car."

III.

"Apres moi,
le deluge."
— *Madame Pompadour*

WHEN WE HAD settled I came straight to the point. "I want you to rejoin the family, Mary Elizabeth. You have been separated from your kin for too long."

I sipped the coffee. She made it strong and thick, the way the Turks do, no milk or sugar to cut it. I suppose she learned that from her husband.

"I want to get to know my grandson," I said.

"And?"

"And what?"

"I remember you as being more direct, Mother."

"What do you mean?"

"You want us to join our two operations. With our combined output and the distributors each of us has set up, we could supply the entire eastern half of the state. It's just a nice extra that you'll get to know your grandson Angus. Or should I say another of your grandsons named Angus."

"You wrong me."

"Really?" She gulped her coffee, then rolled it around in her mouth. "Don't worry. I had the same idea. I've already sent my guards home, though I doubt you have the storage space to handle all my stock. Which is inventoried by the way, so I'll know how much you've moved." She smiled at me. "And don't look so shocked. You and I both know this should have happened five years ago. But with Nick in the way—well, that's in the past."

"You have pretty cold blood for a widow of two hours."

"I'm a MacKay. I get it naturally."

I was offended by this, of course, but did not let it show.

"How much help will it take to run the operation in this county?"

Mary Elizabeth made a dismissive gesture that would have been a mortal insult from anyone else. "I've been running it for years. Nick was too busy chasing whores. The only thing he contributed was an artist's touch with the mash. And I have his recipes."

"Yes, but you'll be back in Peony Springs. There must be someone here to—"

"I won't be moving to Peony Springs. I've been here fifteen years and I like it just fine," she said. "I'll run my own operations, though I agree that a single central warehouse is more efficient. Only one set of payoffs, one set of guards."

She was smart and a true businesswoman. Be that as it may, I was not getting what I wanted.

"But I want us to be together again," I said.

"I am not moving back into my mother's home just because we're both widows."

I flinched, because that had been exactly my thinking.

"I believe your son would benefit from knowing his cousins, and aunts, and uncles."

"You mean the ones who beat him and threw him in the river to drown? Or the ones who helped lynch his father? I can't see how there will be anything but bad blood between Angus and his Potemkin kin. He'll stay with me and finish school."

She had a point. I tried one last time.

"But I am his grandmother. Do I not deserve to know him?"

"You can visit here if you like. Be sure to call ahead and check that we'll be home," she said. "I see this as a business transaction between former competitors." She finished her coffee and threw the dregs out the window. "And it may not last that long, if I read the signs right."

"Must it be like this?"

"Don't misunderstand me, Mother. This isn't about you. It's just that I don't think Prohibition is going to last much longer. The Great Experiment hasn't turned out so great. I think the politicians are just looking for an excuse to overturn the Volstead Act."

"You better hope that you are wrong. Our fortune rests on the act."

"We should be planning now for the way to run our business the day after it's repealed."

I have often noted that the MacKay women are both the strength and the curse of the family. Mary Elizabeth had been hot as a pistol growing up. As a grown woman she was going to be as headstrong as before.

She looked at me sharply. Clearly she had still something on her mind.

"Is that Jackie Sue related to my boy? Because if I know

Angus, they had more than hands inside each other's clothes. We may need to fix her problem. I don't want to be raising some inbred idgit."

I blanched. My daughter was already a step ahead of me.

BIG BILL SYKES REVEALED

Zeus does not bring
all men's plans to fulfillment.
— *Homer*

I.

"I'VE TALKED WITH Governor Fuller and he has appointed me to head a task force to root out these thorns of intolerance, these weeds of prejudice from the soil of our fair state." I looked the reporter directly in the eyes. It was time to put into practice my understanding of the psychology of the press. "I can give you a complete copy of my prepared statement, Miss Freeman."

"You can call me Gwendolyn, Mr. Sykes," she said, and I think there was more than reportorial interest in her gaze.

"Then you must call me Big Bill. Everybody in the county does."

"The name of Big Bill Sykes will be known across the state once this story hits the paper."

"That's very kind of you to say so. I am here to serve the people." I opened my humidor. "Do you mind if I smoke, Gwendolyn? I find it helps my concentration and there are a number of details to arrange. I want this plan in action as soon as possible."

"Go ahead. I love the smell of a good cigar. I'd have a hard time covering politics if I didn't." She bent over her notebook and reviewed her notes. A few moments later she lifted her head and sniffed. "And those smell wonderful. In fact, I've come to enjoy a smoke myself."

I started at that. This woman bore watching. I let her withdraw one of my Belicosos, and watched her savor its aroma. She took my proffered clipper and expertly prepared the head for lighting, then licked the other end, in what I can only describe as a lascivious manner. She finished her performance—and I now see that's what it was—by delicately biting off the tip.

I handed her a Lucifer and watched her wave it properly before firing the Cuban. She puffed it to life and drew in a mouthful of smoke. I did the same with mine and we exhaled mutually.

"Since the Klan seems to be so ensconced in your hometown, won't that be a problem come re-election time?"

"Can I speak off the record?"

She nodded and made some notes.

"I doubt that I will be involved in local politics any longer. I've had my sights set on state office for some time. I've been in touch with the Boston Democrats and they like my stance in opposing anti-Catholic prejudice."

She smiled. "Watch yourself, Big Bill. Those boys play rough."

"I can take care of myself." I set my cigar aside and pulled my papers together. "Did the photographer want to get a last shot for the afternoon papers?"

"Joe left a while ago. He had to get back to have the film developed in time." She inhaled deeply. "Say, do you mind if I just park myself in the corner and finish this beauty? Some people don't approve of seeing a lady smoke. You can just do your work and pretend I'm not here."

"Perhaps we can have a bite of lunch later," I

said, nodding assent. I had hopes for a postprandial delight.

She pushed her chair back against the wall and began to write longhand in her notebook. I started to think how best to publicize my campaign.

Just then my office door jerked open and Granny MacKay stormed in, looking as if lightning might shoot from her eyes.

"Do I not always pay on time, Sykes? Have I ever once not contributed to your political fund?"

I didn't like the tone of this, or where it might be headed, and I put up my hand to stop her. I felt like King Canute trying to hold back the tide.

"That damned militia broke up my stills. They took axes to fifty barrels of my best stuff. I was aging my rye for a change, hoping to attract the upscale trade away from Kennedy's bootleggers."

I knew all this. It had been at my order. It was part of my horse trading to get the governor to let me use the militia. And of course it would be another proof of my reform credentials.

I glanced desperately over at Miss Freeman. She was writing so fast I thought her notebook might catch fire. I rose to my feet and went around my desk to escort Granny from the room. I took her elbow.

"Mrs. MacKay, I have a guest—"

"Take your hand from my person if you know what is good for you. MacKays do not take kindly to the mistreatment of their women."

I dropped her elbow, but tried to crowd her toward the door using my size.

"You're right. Destruction of private property is an

outrage." I got her through the door. "Let's find Marshal Lawe and see what can be done."

From the corner of my eye I saw Gwendolyn snatch her pocketbook from the floor and hurry after us. I hustled Granny toward the courthouse entry.

And whom should we meet but Marshal Lawe, with Eugene and Martha Palmer on *his* coattails, looking mournful.

The marshal and I stepped aside to talk privately. I could see Granny move to her nephew and his wife. She was still bristling, but seemed concerned about whatever had brought her relatives down to the courthouse.

And of course the reporter was right beside them, all ears.

"We got us more of a situation than I thought, Big Bill," said Lawe. "And I thought what we had was bad enough."

"I know. I already heard the militia went after Granny's stills and warehouse."

This took Lawe by surprise.

"I told them to stay away from her stuff," he said. He gave me a sideways look. "Course, they're part of your special investigation team, aren't they?"

I just nodded, waiting to see what else he had. I hadn't let Lawe in on my plans. I had been hoping to scoop him up in the general investigation at a later date.

"But that ain't what I was talking about." He hooked a thumb at Eugene and Martha. "Jackie Sue has gone missing."

I felt like I do when I try to take an extra step on the staircase.

"When?"

"They can't say for sure, but sometime after ten last night."

We both thought about the timing of that; the militiamen chasing through the woods, the Klan running in disarray, the lynching of Nick DeCosta, and the murder of Jedediah Spout.

"Young people run off sometimes," I said.

"I know that. We've asked around, checked with all her school friends. Nothing. Checked with anybody who might have been on the streets early in the morning. No girl was seen walking the roads, either in town or out."

I could feel a throbbing behind my right eye. I needed an aspirin and a drink.

Lawe went on. "Since the militia is part of your special investigation team, I was hoping we could get a building by building search, make sure she's not just hiding somewhere."

I saw the chance to mollify Granny and her kin by taking quick and decisive action. Lawe and I spent the next ten minutes setting things in motion, putting Lieutenant Able in charge. I foisted Eugene and Martha onto Granny and got all of them out of my hair. Granny promised we weren't finished yet.

I ground my teeth when the reporter stayed behind to get the whole story.

II.

"...and oozy weeds about me twist."
Billy Budd, Foretopman
— Herman Melville

LAWE AND I repaired to Gladys' diner, across the street from the courthouse. I poured myself coffee, added a generous shot from my hip flask, and asked if Gladys might have an aspirin handy.

She just glared at me and pointed to a sign. "We reserve the right to refuse service to anyone," she said. "Get out."

Lawe and I both gaped.

"Gladys, what's got into you?" said Lawe. "Why you want to insult Big Bill like that?"

"You think I don't know you were behind that Klan rally last night, Sykes?" Her glance could have blistered my skin.

Lawe said, "You don't want to start making libelous accusations, Gladys."

"I know what I'm talking about. That damn Kleagle came by yesterday with a note for Sykes. I can put two and two together. Just takes common sense."

Lawe looked troubled and he stared into his coffee like he hoped there was an answer there.

Gladys suddenly burst into tears. "And now he's gone."

"Nick DeCosta?" I said.

"Jedediah Spout?" Lawe said.

Gladys waved her hand in a despairing gesture. She wiped away her tears with the dishtowel she always had tucked into the waistband of her apron.

"No. My colored dishwasher, Darnell."

And there went my chance for the colored vote.

Gladys sobbed again and choked out. "That bastard Jedediah said he didn't want any harm to come to him, but now Darnell's disappeared."

Lawe stood up. He grabbed his hat from the rack by the door and said, "I better make up a detail of militiamen to search the woods. We got two missing people now. Jackie Sue, white thirteen-year-old female, and Darnell, colored adult male."

I felt the blood drain from my face.

If this was what it looked like, my career was at an end.

EULALA RESTORED

There is no worse lie
than a truth misunderstood
by those who hear it.
The Varieties of Religious Experience
— *William James*

I.

I HAD BEEN so fired up when I left the farm that I hadn't worn proper shoes or even a coat. Making my way into the woods where I expected to meet Jed, my feet were now blistered and bruised. My legs had been switched by brambles and there was streaks of blood from my knees on down. Plus I was taking a chill.

When I saw the glow from a fire I went over to warm myself. There were two hobos standing there. Yarning and spitting, if I knew 'bos.

They seemed a bit touched, but they were able to point me in the right direction to find my husband. I took it as a sign I was doing the right thing.

I took that last quarter mile extra slow and quiet. I could smell the charred flesh above the sweet odor of the night forest.

I needed to see what Jedediah was up to and decide how to handle him. I knew I wouldn't get but one chance.

There was still a small fire burning below the hanged man. Jedediah sat on his haunches, seeming to be deep in thought peering at something above the body.

I moved in absolute silence to a spot behind a tree off to his left. It was no more than eight or nine yards and I was certain I could hit him in the temple. A good hard blow there should kill him. If not, it would at least knock him out and I would, I would, I—

If I didn't kill him with one marble from my sling, was I really capable of killing him up close? And with what?

I remembered that Jed always had a pocketknife on him, but I wasn't sure I could cut his throat and watch him bleed to death.

No, I needed this to be one clean shot, a sure kill.

I took the sling from my pocket and fitted the elastic. I plucked out three marbles and inspected them, letting what little firelight there was glint off the surface of each. There was an aggie, a steelie, and a cat's eye.

I kept the cat's eye. I put it in my mouth and covered it good with spit, because my grandfather told me human spit makes the shot run true from a sling. I don't know if he schooled all his granddaughters this way, but I was glad to recall his advice.

I breathed in and out slowly, letting the anger turn from jitters to strength and calm.

I put the marble in the pouch. I pulled back, aiming with care.

I took a deep breath, let it half out and held it.

Just as I let the marble fly a gunshot rang out and Jedediah jerked his head to look for its source.

Instead of hitting him in the temple, the marble went straight into his left eye. He gave a sharp gasp, clutched his hands to his face and fell to the ground. His body twitched for some seconds and then grew still.

Something black fell from above and fluttered to the ground.

I kept holding my breath, until I had to let go. I drew air ragged, but as quiet as I could.

Who had fired that shot? What was that thing that fell to earth?

I stayed hidden in the shadows.

II.

Boast not thyself of tomorrow;
for thou knowest not
what a day bring forth.
— *Proverbs 27:1*

I HEARD STEPS, slow and stealthy. A Negro man stepped into the clearing. He made his way to Jed and stared down at him, watching to see if Jed was breathing. He bent over and put his fingers against Jed's neck, checking the pulse.

He turned in a circle, checking the edge of the clearing, looking to see if someone else was there. When he faced my way I could see the whites showing all around his eyes.

"Who there?" he said. "I know someone there. I know someone else killed this man."

I held my silence.

"I been waiting here half an hour, thinking I goin' to kill this man. But I didn't do it, no. 'Stead, I killed the fetch," he gestured to the black thing on the ground, and then to the hanging corpse. "Keep it from taking this poor soul to hell."

"What's a fetch?" I called from the shadows, figuring he still couldn't see me.

Faster than I would have thought possible the Negro

had jumped to a spot right beside me. We stared at each other at close range.

He was breathing hard and I could smell the fear on him. I could see from his eyes he thought my appearance gruesome.

"Who you?" he said.

"You first."

"My name Darnell."

"Eulala Spou'."

"Spout? That your husband?"

I said nothing. He looked at the sling in my hand. He took me by the wrist and pulled me over to Jedediah's body.

"He dead. Why?"

"See my face? He hit me today. Not for the first time. Tonight I hit him back."

I bent down to look close. I smelt that Jed had fouled himself.

I guess that isn't just an old wive's tale.

The marble had burst Jed's left eye on its way into his brain. Some kind of jelly-like stuff was running down his face.

"Yeah, you hit him back and now he dead. But I'm a Negro in the vicinity and I gots a gun. They gonna blame me. They gonna hunt me down and then I be the black fruit hanging from this tree."

I saw the injustice in his predicament.

"Not if they don't know he's dead," I said.

"What you mean?"

"Let's drag his body off somewhere, bury it. People will be so distracted by this man hanging here, no one will think to go looking for Jed."

He looked unbelieving.

"I sure won't tell anyone he's missing. Why would anyone think to look?"

I marveled that I could think so clearly in this situation. And it was another marvel that I felt this unknown Negro was my ally.

IT WAS SETTLED and we went about it. It was harder work than we had thought. Jed's a larger than average man. I couldn't lift him, not even half of him. Plus a body is awkward to move, arms and legs going every which way, the head bumping around.

In the end we each grabbed a foot and dragged him. We went as far as we were able. Well, I guess as far as I was able. Probably half a mile or so. We found a ravine and tumbled Jed over the edge, letting gravity get him to the bottom.

Darnell put the rifle over his shoulder. "You never gonna see this nigger again. Nobody in this town ever gon' see me. I be a black ghost."

He took off into the forest at a trot and disappeared from my view in moments.

I don't know why, but as I stood there I thought about the farm and whether I could work it by myself.

The moon chose that moment to come out from behind the clouds and lit up Jed's face at the bottom of the ravine like a searchlight.

That won't do at all.

I made my way to the floor of the gulley.

It took half an hour to get him covered. I had no tools and there wasn't a lot of loose soil in the ravine. I was exhausted and knew I still had a two and a half hour walk back to the farm.

I took the easy way and covered him with as deep a layer of leaves as I could. When I climbed back to the rim of the ravine, I looked to see if Jed was visible.

The bottom of the ravine was black as the pit of hell.

Just right for him.

CHIEF REVIVED

> ...and let none
> presume on his good fortune until he find
> Life, at his death, a memory without pain.
> *Oedipus Rex*
> — *Sophocles*

I.

CHIEF WAKE. HEAD still hurt. Night, cold. Chief not remember this place. What is place? Why Chief here? Chief remember nothing.

Chief stand. Chief sick, throw food from mouth. Chief sniff food on ground. Chief not eat.

Chief lost. Chief smart dog, follow Chief trail back to home.

Chief run through forest, fast-fast. Trail clear, follow easy. Sometime Chief run into tree. Why? Not happen before.

Chief come to bad place. Smell fear, smell death, smell burned meat. Chief find Kaw on ground.

Kaw dead. Good, Kaw dead, Chief happy.

Wind blow. Chief see something move over Chief head. Look up.

No! Bad thing. Man dead. Man move in wind.

Chief remember, remember Chief eat man-meat. Remember Chief ashamed, want die.

Chief look down. Chief not want remember.

Chief see new thing, see track on ground. Man and man-bitch drag dead man. Why?

Chief follow track. Easy. Chief good hunter. Follow track to rocky place. Chief smell dead man on rocks, follow smell.

Chief go down in rocks. Smell man who hit Chief in head, not see man. Dig in leaves.

There! Man who hit Chief, dead man. Grrrr.

Chief show angry teeth. Dead man make Chief not remember, make Chief head hurt. Dead man make Chief ashamed, make Chief hide in forest.

Chief angry. Chief growl.

Chief attack.

Two News Items
and
A Letter Home

SEARCH CALLED OFF
September 6, 1929—
Peony Springs

Marshal Ichabod Lawe, 34, said that the search for Darnell Boggs, 32, Negro male, has been suspended. Boggs, who has several prior criminal convictions, had been implicated in the August 24 disappearance of Jackie Sue Palmer, 14.

"Her family received a letter from Jackie Sue this week indicating that she has not been abducted, but has sought work outside the county," reported Marshal Lawe. "We have issued a bulletin to the surrounding counties that Boggs is no longer a suspect in any crime."

The exact whereabouts of Miss Palmer remain unknown.

PROSECUTOR RECALLED
September 26, 1929—
Peony Springs

Potemkin County Prosecutor William "Big Bill" Sykes, 31, was removed from office in a recall election this past Tuesday. Sykes now faces corruption charges stemming from the indictment that he accepted bribes from illegal distilleries so that he would ignore their violation of Prohibition.

Sykes is remembered for having begun a crusade against the KKK in western Massachusetts. It now appears he may have been complicit in allowing the local klavern to lynch Nicolas DeCosta, who was a key witness in an attempted murder case. Herman Schneider, the County Public Defender, says that Mr. Sykes was losing the case at the time of the lynching.

Marshal Ichabod Lawe, 34, head of law enforcement in Peony Springs, issued a statement: "There is no room for this kind of twisted justice in our town. We believe in family values here, and we toss out those who don't."

October 20, 1929
Hollywood!

Dear Ma and Pa and Bros.,

I hope this finds you well. I am doing fine and my career is going great guns. The movies is where I was always meant to be. Though I've learned a few things about show business, I'll tell you.

I know you don't go to the movies that much, but if you was to see the latest Clara Bow film there's a part where her maid brings a tray with coffee and cookies. Well, I'm the maid! My name isn't in the list of players, but I feel I'm on my way! I have pretty steady work now as an extra.

I am sorry not to have written since September, but life is awful full on a movie set, what with a call time of five in the A.M. Then getting into the day's costume, maybe a school girl, or an Indian Princess, or a maid, as I said before. Plus make up and hair dressing.

Then the assistant director tells us extras what we have to do next, and finally the cameras roll and they take our picture.

Come lunch time I usually take a walk around the studio cuz I'm watching my figure. More of the same in the afternoon.

At night there's parties and the extras get invited same as the stars. I've met Fattie Arbuckel and Mack Sinnitt and Harry Lloyd and tons of others. They're all just regular guys!

Anyway, I thought I'd right you cuz I feared you might be feeling blue with your girl gone from home for so long.

I didn't put my address in case you still had thoughts of finding me and bringing me back to Peony Springs.

Ever Your Daughter
JSP

P.S. Also I changed my name. The agent told me Jackie Sue Palmer would never sell any tickets.

LAWE'S LAST RIPOSTE

I.

SOME SAY THAT I'm quarrelsome and a gossip. I maintain I'm just interested in the truth, which I have found to be slippery. Looked at one way, something might seem to be true and just. Looked at another it may be harmful.

It was a boon to justice in our county when Big Bill Sykes was removed from office, him being corrupt and all. On the other hand it made the public defender recall several trials he thought had gone the wrong way and they were tried again. Of course it was the taxpayers who bore the brunt of that brainstorm.

Three men even got released from prison, to the joy of their families. It also delighted their drinking buddies who had got them into trouble in the first place. It took no more than six months for all three to be re-incarcerated.

And of course Judge Halbertson made another rotten play on words saying they must have thought they were gonna be reincarnated, they seemed so eager to return to their wicked ways.

Suzy Ann had lost her best client, but soon found others to replace Big Bill. She made something of a name for herself by trying to sell a line of special treatment cigars, if you know what I mean. She couldn't produce them in the numbers her clients requested, so she opened a sweat shop in Boston and hired Sicilian girls right off the boat.

When she finally got busted the records she kept of who her clients was turned out to be her best defense. She did thirty days and then moved somewhere west, where the laws wasn't quite so strict. Texas, I think I heard.

Granny MacKay and Mary Elizabeth joined operations and took over the hooch business for the western half of the state, and they weren't any too ladylike about it. They left a trail of broken bones and bloody heads, but always outside my jurisdiction. Shows Kipling knew what he was talking about when he said the female of the species is deadlier than the male.

I tried to court Mary Elizabeth, but she wasn't having it. Plus I couldn't abide spending more'n ten minutes at a time with her peacock of a son.

Darnell Boggs was never seen in Peony Springs again. However, Gladys did allow as how she'd heard he was back in Virginia and staying out of trouble. I never quite understood her interest in that boy, or how she got word.

Ebeneezer Kauz and Lars Gunnarsen was found froze to death that fall. They'd been drinkin' something cheaper than usual and it left them senseless while they was campin'. The temperature dropped and that was all she wrote. The city planted the both of 'em in the same pauper's grave.

It's still an open case as to who killed Jedediah Stout. And also who tore his face up. I have my suspicions, but nothing solid ever came of it. His widow Eulala sold the farm and moved to another town.

And Jackie Sue, the start of all this? Ain't she a wonder? I actually saw her in a moving picture show.

There she was dressed up like an Injun gal, standing next to a teepee. She got shot and died when the cavalry rode up, and she done a great job of it, took her about twenty seconds before she finally went to her reward.

Chief had showed up with a bad head wound and some broken ribs, which I figure he got fighting the klux. He still wanted to be the best dog cop in Potemkin County, but he didn't have the strength he used to.

And on occasion he'd go crazy barking at some fool crow. Well, I still loved that dog, so I found jobs he could do.

I don't believe I ever had a case that caused me to wax so philosophical. I don't think it harms a man to do so.

I find myself talking late into the night with Gladys, something I enjoy almost as much as her cookin', which is as good as anything I ever et.

Seems our talk turns more and more to our future. What with the world at peace and times being fairly prosperous, things look hopeful.

Marshal Lawe
October 21, 1929

AFTERWORD

This was an exciting novel to write. Interviewing those whose memory stretched back to the 1920s was opening a window into an extraordinary period of US history.

The Twenties were Roaring indeed. Bootleg gin was both illegal and readily available. All the neighborhood bars and pubs had been closed, to be replaced by up to six times as many speak-easies. Jazz was transforming popular music. More and more homes had radios. The Amos 'n' Andy show debuted on the Blue Network.

The economy was booming, but agricultural prices fell rapidly after the war. The foreclosure rate on farms rose steadily throughout the decade, skyrocketing with the 1929 depression.

By the end of World war I, nearly five million men and women had served in the US forces. With the League of Nations' promise of no more war, the standing US Army was reduced to 38,000. The veterans were dumped into the workplace. Unions suffered setbacks because of the huge influx of labor.

Those veterans who had seen the women and brothels of Europe also had a new sensibility toward death. They wanted to live life and they wanted to live it now.

Returning Negro veterans understood their service as having earned them full citizenship. They had new skills and they wanted better jobs. Racial tensions ran high.

The Spanish Influenza killed over 600,000 Americans, and perhaps fifty million people worldwide. My great-uncle was one of them. He got on a train to go to Detroit for a job and died within the day. To combat the spread of the flu he was buried immediately. No one from his family was there.

The number of cars in America rose from eight million in 1920 to twenty-three million in 1930. There was enough room inside those cars to seat every American alive at the time.

Flappers transformed the sexual mores of the era. They were depicted in plays, on billboards, in magazine ads, and in the libertine movies of the day. They were a slap in the face to conventional morality and conservative America. There wouldn't be another sexual revolution of this magnitude until the 1960s.

Immigration, nearly impossible during the war, began again. The largest groups were from Southern and Eastern Europe. As with all previous immigrants, they were deeply resented by those groups already established here.

In 1915 the Klan was reestablished in Georgia. Rather than remaining a southern phenomenon, it was organized on a nationwide basis, with klaverns in nearly every state of the union. I have been shocked to find how many people I know had family that was in the Klan in the 1920s.

Although this is a novel, nearly every incident is based on an actual event. My job was to weave a tapestry that gives the reader a sense of life in rural New England during that turbulent decade, while telling a mystery tale.

Finally, I have been saddened to find that much of the history of the KKK needs to be updated. I discovered things that I chose not to use in this novel, for fear they wouldn't be believed.

The Klan has changed names, but still survives in more places than I would have thought possible before I began this journey. The Southern Poverty Law Center Intelligence Report for Spring 2007 lists 844 active hate groups in the United States, including 165 Ku Klux Klan klaverns in 35 states.